THE GROWTH MINDSET
WORKBOOK FOR
TEENS

CBT & DBT Skills to Grow in
Self-Confidence, Build Resilience,
and Overcome Life's Challenges

Written By: Empower Teens

CONTENTS

FREE BONUS CONTENT!

As a way of saying thank you for purchasing our workbook, we're offering 4 free bonus content!

To access the content, scan this QR code by using the camera on your phone and click on the link that appears

Or enter this url in your web browser:
bit.ly/empower-teens

(only use lower case letters)

INTRODUCTION

I wish someone had taught me about a growth mindset when I was in school. It would've helped me SO much in my life. It took me a bit longer to stumble upon this little secret that really isn't a secret. And then it completely changed my life.

It didn't happen overnight. Nothing really does, right? What's that saying? *"Rome wasn't built in a day."* Cheesy, I know. But it's true.

I've learned that nothing worthwhile comes easy. That the things that matter take a lot of work, and the things that don't take work don't seem to matter that much.

You've been granted this amazing opportunity called life, and you get to choose how you want to live it. It will be the greatest adventure and you will get to do so many things. And if you choose to do it whilst cultivating a growth mindset, you'll have an even better life.

The aim of this book is to provide you with the knowledge to empower yourself with the skills, tools, and strategies you need for this life that lies ahead of you. Each chapter is filled with valuable information and insights into what it takes to foster a growth mindset for the rest of your life.

Never again will you see a failure as a failure. Never again will you talk about yourself in a negative manner. Once you've worked through this book you, and only you will hold the key to your future. You'll have the tools and the know-how to embark on the adventure that is your self-growth and self-development.

Treat this book like any other workbook. Read it through once, then come back to it again and again. Do the exercises, then review the content again. This should become your playbook for life.

In these pages I teach you how to deal with setbacks, how to grow your confidence, how to grow your skills, how to set effective goals for yourself and step-by-step instructions on how to achieve those goals.

If you read nothing else in your life, at least just read this book. I promise you that it will open your eyes to a new world. A world where you are in control of your own destiny.

Now, let the journey begin.

CHAPTER 1

LET'S TALK FOUNDATIONS

"You can't build a great building on a weak foundation" - Gordon B. Hinkley

What does a "growth mindset" mean exactly?

Well, let me ask you another question. Do you think you can raise your own IQ? Or do you believe that you are born with a certain IQ level and that it cannot be changed? How you answer these two questions will determine whether you have a growth mindset or a fixed mindset. If you answered yes to the first question, you have a growth mindset. It then follows that if you agreed more with the second question, you have a fixed mindset.

A growth mindset is a belief that you can improve your skills and increase your intelligence through effort, planning, and practice.

Maybe you're not good at sports? You've never been good at sports so you don't even try anymore. Let's take baseball as an example. What do you think would happen if you spent just 20 minutes a day, Monday through Friday, in the batting cage? Some people would say that it doesn't matter how much effort or practice you put in. If you're not born with an innate ability to play sports, you're just not cut out for it and should rather focus on academics. Though, in reality, we've learned that if you spend just 100 hours a year focusing on a certain skill, it would make you better than 95% of others at that particular skill. That equates to just 18 minutes a day!

Past generations believed that you are born with certain skills and aptitudes that you could not acquire any other way. Like your IQ for example. When I say IQ I'm referring to your "intelligence quotient" as there are different types of intelligence. You get emotional intelligence, mathematical intelligence, linguistics intelligence, and many more. In the past, people believed that you couldn't change your IQ. If you were born with an IQ of 100, it would remain 100 until the day you die.

I can tell you from personal experience that this isn't true. I learned about this thing called the Mensa High IQ Society early on in my life and always wanted to try out to become a member. It's an international society of the top 2% of people around the world with the highest IQs. To become a member you need to write two different IQ tests and score in the 98th percentile.[1]

I would bet money on the fact that if you asked people on the street whether you could increase your score on an IQ test, most people would say no, right? Have you ever heard of someone studying for an IQ test? Well, I decided to test it out. I took an online test and documented my score. Then I went online and downloaded the questions and answers to multiple online IQ tests. I spent some time studying each one and then took the test again. This time my score went up exponentially. Then I went and wrote the Mensa IQ test and was accepted as a member.

This tells me two things.

1. You shouldn't place so much importance on the score you receive on an IQ test as it's a pretty crude measuring system.
2. You can improve your "perceived" intelligence through studying.

This basically means that it doesn't matter whether you're not the best baseball player when you start out. With enough time, dedication, and practice, you can build up the skills of a pro player.

On the opposite end of the spectrum is someone who holds a fixed mindset. This person wasn't born with ball skills and they also don't believe that they can learn or improve their ball skills. They have slow reflexes, lack hand-eye coordination, and have little to no muscle mass to even throw a ball. They limit themselves to believing that they've been dealt a bad hand when it comes to athletics and probably won't even try out at all.

As you may imagine, holding on to a fixed mindset can be pretty limiting with all kinds of consequences throughout your life. If you hold on to the belief that you are not capable of learning new skills or improving the skills you already possess, what does that mean for your future? It probably means that you won't get very far, or will settle for living a life that you're not entirely happy with.

No one is born a pro. It takes practice, failing, learning, and some more practice to get good at anything in life. Even if you have excellent reflexes and above-average ball skills, you still need to practice to become a pro baseball player. You still need to put in the time and effort of playing hundreds of games before you get signed as a pro.

Everyone struggles in life. Everyone has to face challenges and failure. If you choose (and it is a choice) to adopt a growth mindset, you choose to view challenges and failures as learning opportunities, rather than deficiencies or a sign that you're a disappointment. That's exactly what failure is. It's just feedback teaching us what not to do, so we can try something in a different way.

You might know the famous example of Thomas Eddison who was asked in an interview how he felt about his many failures before finally succeeding in creating the first lightbulb. To which he replied: *"I have not failed. I have just found 10 000 ways that won't work."* [2]

Imagine if he had given up after the first 10 or 100 tries.

Imagine if Michael Jordan, one of the best basketball players, is a prime example of what it means to adopt a growth mindset. In an interview, he said: *"I've missed more than 9,000 shots in my career. I've lost almost 300 games. Twenty-six times I've been trusted to take the game-winning shot and missed. I've failed over and over and over again in my life. And that is why I succeed."* [3]

People who choose to adopt a growth mindset are statistically more successful in their lives than those who choose to adopt a fixed mindset. I mean, it just makes sense. If you don't believe that you can do better, you won't.

You become what you think about the most. So if you constantly put yourself down and think that you are a loser, or that you're not good enough, or that you'll never be successful - you're right. If you constantly choose to think about how grateful you are for the opportunities and blessings in your life, no matter how small, and how successful you'll be in life - you're also right.

This is why it's so important that you be very careful about what thoughts you allow yourself to focus on. More often than not, we cause ourselves to fail because we focus so much on thoughts of us failing. It is why top athletes are taught how to visualize themselves winning all the time.

Here are a few more examples of a growth mindset vs a fixed mindset:

EXAMPLE 1

Yesterday, Tim's mother, who is a famous artist, was trying to teach him how to draw a realistic face. Though Tim really struggled to get the proportions right and it ended up looking "Picasso"-like.

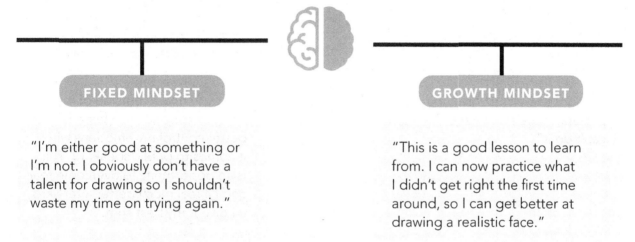

FIXED MINDSET

"I'm either good at something or I'm not. I obviously don't have a talent for drawing so I shouldn't waste my time on trying again."

GROWTH MINDSET

"This is a good lesson to learn from. I can now practice what I didn't get right the first time around, so I can get better at drawing a realistic face."

Tip: Rather than give up immediately after just one try, encourage yourself to give it another go. Remind yourself of some of the people you look up to. I can assure you none of them gave up after just trying something once. When we don't get something right, it's just an opportunity for us to learn from. It'll get better with practice.

EXAMPLE 2

I am terrified of speaking in public and next week we have to present a talk on the career we wish to pursue in class. I don't know how I'm going to manage.

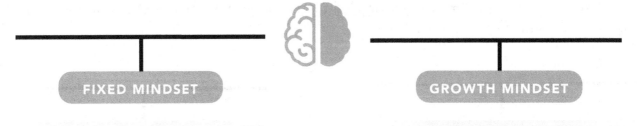

FIXED MINDSET

"I might as well just give up or pretend to be sick on the day. I just can't do it"

GROWTH MINDSET

"I'll push myself outside of my comfort zone so I can learn how to better control my emotions when it comes to public speaking. This is an opportunity to overcome fear and I'll feel much better afterward if I give it my best shot."

Tip: Sometimes we get so caught up in our emotions that we lose sight of the fact that this might present us with an excellent learning opportunity. Besides, it's just a few minutes. If you can be brave for just a few minutes and give it your best, you will have conquered your fear and can feel proud of yourself for showing up even when you really didn't want to.

EXAMPLE 3

Deshawn is struggling to throw a football as well as he could, so the coach gives him some constructive criticism on how he can improve.

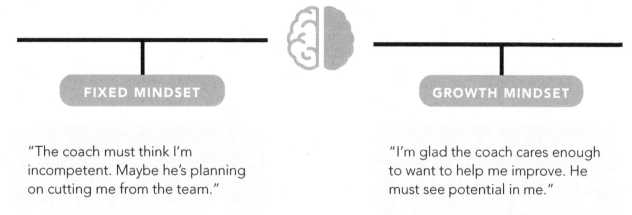

FIXED MINDSET

"The coach must think I'm incompetent. Maybe he's planning on cutting me from the team."

GROWTH MINDSET

"I'm glad the coach cares enough to want to help me improve. He must see potential in me."

Tip: When people give you feedback, including constructive criticism, try and see it for what it is. They care enough to want to help you improve. If they didn't care about you they wouldn't have said anything in the first place. [4]

The main point I'd like to express in this first chapter is that you have a choice. Even though we might not be in control of every little thought that pops into our heads, we do have a choice when it comes to which thoughts we continue to focus on. I might have a thought pop into my head saying: "You're not good at this, just give up." If I choose to focus on that thought, I am giving up my own power and allowing the negative thought to win.

There's a great example that went around a few years ago and it goes something like this. Your mind is a garden and you need to tend to it on a daily basis. All those niggly, negative thoughts that pop into your head are like weeds. The positive and empowering thoughts are the healthy, indigenous flowers and plants in your garden. If you don't tend to the weeds by pulling them out and throwing them away, they'll take over your garden.

The moral of the story is that you are capable of far more than you might believe you are. I'm not saying that reaching any level of success is easy. What I am saying is that it is possible for anyone who is willing to try. Anyone who is willing to put in the effort and believe in themselves will always be better off than someone who decides that they're not worth it.

You are worth it!

EXERCISE

Spend some time thinking about the type of mindset you hold. Write down some examples of beliefs that you hold that relate to both a fixed mindset and a growth mindset. Try and write down at least 3 examples for each.

CHAPTER 2

NEUROPLASTICITY

"Because of the power of neuroplasticity, you can, in fact, reframe your world and rewire your brain so that you are more objective. You have the power to see things as they are so that you can respond thoughtfully, deliberately, and effectively to everything you experience." - Elizabeth Thornton

Your brain is plastic.

Okay not literally. How weird would that be, right? I'm referring to a scientific term used in the world of neuroscience. In this instance, plastic means: malleable or having the ability to be shaped or molded. It basically means that your brain is adaptable.

For the longest time, scientists believed that the brain is a fixed structure and that the brain we are born with is the brain we'll die with. Thanks to technological advancements and more studies being conducted in the field of neuroscience, we now know that this isn't true. Your brain has the ability to change. In order for us to understand how this works, we first need to understand the different structures of the brain and their functions.

Your brain is quite literally a supercomputer. It is one of, if not the most complex organ to exist. For many years scientists have been fascinated by the inner workings of this mysterious organ of ours. Thanks to the technological age and ever-advancing scientific equipment and study methods, we are starting to gain a better understanding of how the brain works. Note the emphasis is on the word "starting". Although we've come a long way, we still have a lot to learn.

To better understand how the brain works, we need to have a look at its structures and their individual functions. Don't worry, my aim here is not to throw highly scientific words at you.

My aim is for you to gain a better understanding of how your personal supercomputer works, and how it affects everything in your life. So I'll try to keep it as simple as possible.

THREE MAIN PARTS OF THE BRAIN

The brain is divided into three main parts:

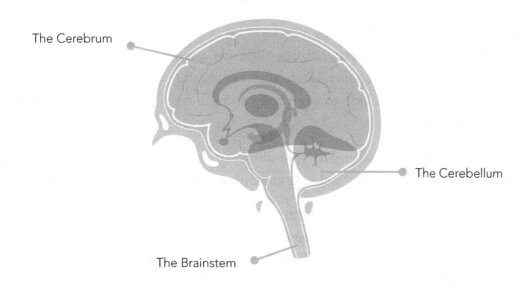

The Cerebrum

The Cerebellum

The Brainstem

THE CEREBRUM: This is the largest part of your brain. It is divided into a left and right hemisphere, which just means a left and right side. All the more complex or higher functions that you need to perform on a daily basis are controlled by this part of the brain. Examples of higher functions include speech, reasoning, thinking, interpreting touch, emotions, learning, fine motor control, and vision and hearing.

THE CEREBELLUM: This part of the brain is situated under the cerebrum and at the back of your brain. It is the older part of our brain. As we have evolved over hundreds of thousands of years, the Cerebrum started developing from and on top of this part of the brain. It controls basic functions like muscle movement, maintaining posture, and balance.

THE BRAINSTEM: This part of the brain acts as the messenger and then relays information between the cerebrum and the cerebellum to the spinal cord. It is probably the oldest part of your brain that first developed and controls functions that are crucial for our survival like breathing, heart rate, swallowing, digestion, sleep cycles, and more.

Now we know that the brain has three main parts and each of these parts is responsible for different functions in our bodies. Imagine looking at the brain from the top or from the front. The cerebrum, which is the biggest part of your brain on top of the cerebellum and spinal cord, is further divided into two separate hemispheres. The left and the right hemisphere. Maybe you've heard of this before or perhaps someone has told you that you're left or right-brain dominant.

In the middle of these two hemispheres, you have a bundle of fibers that connect the two hemispheres and allow them to communicate with one another. What's interesting is that these two parts of the brain work contralaterally. Meaning they work crisscross. The left part of your brain controls the right side of your body and the right part of your brain controls the left side of your body.

The left side of your brain controls speech, your ability to write, comprehension or your ability to understand, and arithmetic. The right side controls creativity, artistic and musical skills.

To further complicate things, there are certain people who do not fit the conventional mold as their abilities are controlled by the opposite hemisphere. The left hemisphere is responsible for language in 92% of people, for example. Which means 8% of people's brains work the other way around.

This is what makes the brain so complicated because it has the ability to adapt. We're getting to the plastic part in just a bit.

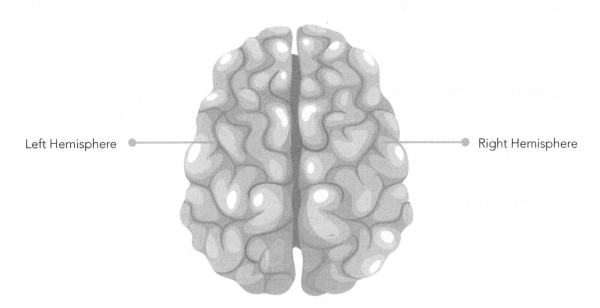

Left Hemisphere   Right Hemisphere

Okay next up, the brain is further divided into four different lobes. I'm sure you're familiar with the terms frontal, temporal, parietal, and occipital lobes.

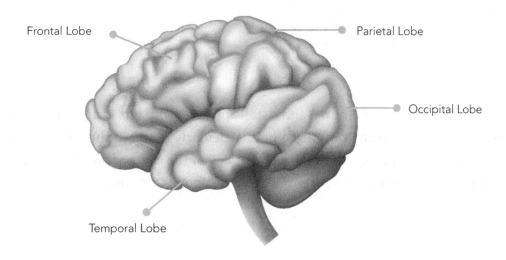

Frontal Lobe: Lies behind your forehead and is responsible for and controls:

- Personality, behavior, and controlling emotions. Your ability to make facial expressions is also controlled in this area.
- Judgment, planning, and problem-solving. Paying attention.
- Speaking and writing. (Controlled by the Broca's area in the frontal lobe)
- Movement.
- Intelligence, concentration, planning, and self-awareness.

Parietal Lobe: This is at the upper rear of your brain and controls the following:

- Interpreting language and words.
- Your sense of touch and ability to sense temperature.
- Interprets sensory information from your environment.
- Spatial and visual perception, as well as body awareness.

Occipital Lobe: Located at the back of your brain and very simply controls and interprets vision.

Temporal Lobe: Is located near your ears and controls and interprets:

- Also, language is controlled by Wernicke's Area and covers both the temporal and parietal lobes.
- Your ability to comprehend spoken language.
- Virtual and visual memory. General knowledge.
- Hearing/ recognizing audio stimuli.
- Organizational skills. [5]

We could go into the deeper structures and details of the brain, but I think that would just be unnecessarily complex information that's not particularly useful in this instance. What I'd rather we explore next is gaining a better understanding of the parts of the brain that controls emotion. This is, after all, what influences our lives the most. Our emotions.

You don't have to be a scientist to understand that emotions have an enormous impact on our lives. Fear can hold us hostage from pursuing our dreams, anger can lead to you losing someone you love or doing something that lands you in trouble. Love can cause you to lose sight of everything else that's going on in your life. Sadness can force you to your knees and cause you to not be able to get out of bed. The point is, our emotions rule our lives. If we allow them to.

Our emotions are driven by our interactions with our environment. Let's say you're at school. You're between classes and need to fetch something from your locker. As you open your locker a scary mask suddenly pops out at you with a bang. You get a fright and what follows is either fear, or anger, or a combination of both. Your interaction (opening your locker) with your environment (the locker and the mask popping out at you) led to an emotional response. At that moment it caused a number of reactions in your body as well, which led to you formulating said emotional response.

Your heart rate went up, your breathing also sped up, and maybe you even noticed that you started sweating in response to being frightened. What causes this?

The simple answer is the limbic system.

The limbic system is a combination of different structures that are located deep inside your brain. These structures are responsible for how you behave and how you feel, emotionally. Although scientists still haven't fully agreed on the different parts that make up the limbic system, it is currently recognized as the following.

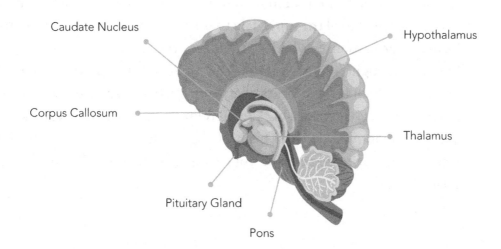

Caudate Nucleus

Hypothalamus

Corpus Callosum

Thalamus

Pituitary Gland

Pons

The Hypothalamus: Is involved in controlling both emotional responses and sexual responses, hormonal release, and regulating your body temperature.

The Hippocampus: Responsible for how you interpret the spatial dimensions of your environment. It is also the area of the brain that helps preserve and retrieve memories.

The Amygdala: A small yet very powerful part of your brain. It is an almond-shaped cluster of cells near the base of your brain that plays an important role in fear and anger. Especially when it comes to the fight or flight response.

The Limbic Cortex: This structure consists of two parts, namely the cingulate gyrus and the parahippocampal gyrus. Combined, they have an impact on your mood, motivation, and judgment.

Okay, I know it's a lot to take in. It is important to have at least a basic understanding of how your brain works because you can't change something without having at least an idea of how it functions. Now we're going to look at which parts of the brain control which emotions. There are hundreds of emotions and going through each is a whole book on its own. So we're just going to focus on four of the main emotions that influence our lives, which are: fear, anger, happiness, and love.

FEAR

Fear is an extremely powerful emotion that can wreak havoc on our lives. It's also an extremely important emotion responsible for our survival and can be particularly helpful in motivating us to progress in life. That small cluster of cells called the Amygdala that I spoke about earlier is responsible for our fear response. When it stimulates the Hippocampus next to it, it initiates the fight/flight response. The Amygdala also plays a role in "fear learning", which is the process of attaching a fear response to certain situations. Let's say you take a big step in telling your crush that you like them and they shoot you down in front of the whole school. That event might lead to you fearing expressing your feelings to anyone else in the future. That's learned fear.

ANGER

Anger is similar to fear in that it is a response to what our brains might perceive as a threat or a stressor in our environment. Just like fear, this response's journey also starts in the Amygdala which stimulates the Hippocampus next to it. Though in addition to this interaction, parts of the prefrontal cortex also come into play. People who have experienced an accident that led to what is known as a Traumatic Brain Injury or "TBI" in this area often have trouble controlling anger and aggression.

HAPPINESS

When you feel happy, you have a positive outlook on life in general. I mean, who wouldn't like to feel more happiness, right? Studies to date suggest that the feeling of happiness originates in the limbic system, which consists of the thalamus, hypothalamus, amygdala, hippocampus, and cingulate gyrus. We're not going to go into each structure.

Another area that plays a role here is a structure known as the Precuneus. This structure is situated in the area of the Parietal lobe and is involved in the processes of retrieving memories, maintaining your sense of self, and focusing your attention as you move around. A study in 2015 found that people who have more gray matter in this area (gray matter is made up of neurons) experienced a greater sense of happiness. [6]

LOVE

And finally, love. As weird as it may sound, the initial forming of the response that we know as "love", actually starts out in the same area where our stress response is triggered in the hypothalamus. I guess it makes sense if you think about how nervous and anxious we feel when we fall in love with someone.

When you hug someone you love, a chemical called "Oxytocin" is released in your brain which gives you that warm, fuzzy feeling. It's also known as the "love hormone". It's produced in your Hypothalamus and released by your Pituitary gland.

Hormones play a vital role in eliciting an emotional response. When it comes to fear, the stress hormones adrenaline and cortisol come into play. Love = dopamine, oxytocin, endorphins, and many more.

Hormones are the regulatory substances within our brain and body that allow us to experience certain emotions. When we go through puberty a change in hormones also takes place to help our bodies change in a way that makes us "adults" and equips us with everything we need for procreation (making babies).

It is these hormones that play havoc on our emotions. It's their fault that you experience mood swings that range from anger to depression and everything in between. Lucky for us it's only temporary. However, you will experience hormonal fluctuations throughout your life. They might not be as intense as puberty (unless you're a woman, in which case you'll have to eventually go through menopause which can be just as intense) but everyone goes through constant hormonal changes.

Though we may not be able to control how these hormones are released, we can control our emotional responses by implementing certain behavioral tools. More on that a bit later. The bottom line is that you should be happy and relieved to know that you are not a slave to your hormones and there is something you can do about it.

It takes getting to know yourself better on a biological level to be able to control your own emotions, mainly because they can be so powerful. Once you understand that emotions are just a sequence of events inside your body that releases certain chemicals, you come to realize that you don't have to buy into automatically reacting to what you're feeling. You can practice certain techniques to change your reactions. You can also change certain structures in your brain. This is where neuroplasticity comes in.

LET'S TALK ABOUT YOUR PLASTIC BRAIN (NEUROPLASTICITY)

Did you know that your brain only reaches full development around the age of 25? That's right, all through school, high school, and even college your brain isn't fully developed yet. It makes sense if you really think about it. There is so much for us to learn on how to navigate this thing called life on Earth, and if you compare that to "what" we are when we are born (I mean how tiny and vulnerable we are) it doesn't really come as a surprise that it would take us so many years to get to a place where our brains have finally learned enough to get to its mature state.

Your brain is actually even better than a supercomputer. You see, your brain can teach itself how to change. A computer cannot do that on its own. A computer cannot tell itself to switch on unless you tell it to do so by using a program. Your brain can!

Now as I mentioned before, the word "plasticity" basically refers to your brain's ability to change and adapt to new experiences.

When you break up the word neuroplasticity you get: "neuro" which refers to neurons, and "plasticity" which means adaptability or ability to be molded.

It took a long time for scientists in general to accept the concept of neuroplasticity. I think this was mainly due to the staggering implications that this theory held.

Although most literature surrounding neuroplasticity refers to 1948 as the year when the term was first used in literature, it actually dates back as far as the early 1900s when Santiago Ramón y Cajal - who is considered the father of neuroscience - first talked about neuronal plasticity.

Then in 1923 American psychologist Karl Lashley conducted experiments on rhesus monkeys that demonstrated changes in neuronal pathways, which he considered to be evidence of neuroplasticity. [7]

Then, in 1948, Polish neuroscientist Jerzy Konorski used the word "neuroplasticity" to describe the process that he also observed which was changes in neuronal structures in the brain.

It wasn't until the 1960s that scientific literature widely adopted the term as more and more evidence came to light that showed that the human brain could change after reaching adulthood. Remember, before then we believed that once you reach a certain age your brain stops developing and that it was impossible to change things like behavior, skills, and cognition after that.

Now we know that neural pathways can, indeed, change and reorganize themselves, causing changes in the physical structures of the brain.

In England, someone who wants to become a cab driver needs to write a test beforehand on all the streets in London. They need to be able to memorize every single road in the city to pass the test. A study was conducted where scientists took brain scans of London taxi drivers before and after they had to write the test. These scans showed that their Hippocampus had gotten larger - the area in your brain associated with memory, remember? (See what I did there?) In patients who have Alzheimer's disease (which leads to symptoms of memory loss and confusion) brain scans showed that the Hippocampus in these patients had shrunk and become damaged. [8]

What this has taught us is that your brain has the ability to change and is not just stuck in one form once it's reached maturity. Different parts of your brain either get bigger or smaller, depending on the activities you choose to engage in.

If it's an activity that demands memory, your Hippocampus will grow. If it's an activity that demands you learn multiple languages it will strengthen your Parietal lobe, etc.

This is exceptionally good news for all of us because it means that we can change the way we think, feel, and behave. It means that we can develop skills and strengthen talents that already exist. We can choose to learn absolutely anything we want because the brain will adapt. More than that, we can choose to learn how to not allow our emotions to impact our behavior in a negative way. With practice, of course. It doesn't happen overnight.

There are 2 types of neuroplasticity:

1. Structural plasticity.
2. Functional plasticity.

STRUCTURAL PLASTICITY

When you are born, you rely on the adults around you for your survival. You don't know how to do anything and need time to develop skills like walking, talking, etc. During the time you spend learning all these skills that are paramount to your survival, your brain is constantly changing., constantly adapting to your environment. This is structural plasticity. [9]

Learning how your behavior and environment (as in the world around you that you interact with, this includes people) influence both the structure and function of your brain will allow you to engage in strategies that lead to living a more "effective" life. This means making conscious choices about the activities and behavior you choose to engage in. Also, the kind of people you choose to surround yourself with when it comes to your friends.

You probably know the saying "Birds of a feather flock together," right? Well turns out it's more than just that. Recent studies have shown that when you are seated near someone who is a high performer, your own performance will go up by 15%. But if you're seated near someone who doesn't care about their performance and engages in toxic traits, your own performance will suffer for it by going down by 30%! Just like "You are what you eat," you also become the people you surround yourself with. [10]

Think about it this way: let's say the behavior of a habit is like a footpath in your brain. For you to engage in said habit, neurons carry the messages needed for you to act out said behavior along a path. If it's a new habit, that path looks like a footpath because you haven't really done it before and the neurons need to learn which route to take to send the information needed to certain parts of your brain. The more you engage in the new habit, the more the neurons travel back and forth along this new path, and the bigger and stronger this path gets. Eventually, it gets to look like a 6-lane highway. That growth in specific areas of your brain is what's known as structural plasticity. This is also why it takes time to form a new habit. The more you do it, the easier it becomes because it's easier for your neurons to travel along a 6-lane highway than an overgrown footpath.

FUNCTIONAL PLASTICITY

Functional plasticity, quite simply, is the brain's ability to take functions from one area of the brain and move it to a different area of the brain when there's been damage to a specific area. So it takes those same functions from the damaged area and moves it to an undamaged area.

There is a famous case in the world of neuroscience and it is the case of a man named Phineas Gage. On September the 13th 1848, Phineas was working as the foreman of a crew cutting a railroad bed. He was using a tamping iron (a crowbar-like tool) to pack explosives into a hole. On this fateful day, the powder detonated and sent the tampering iron - 43 inches long, 1.25

inches in diameter, and weighing 13.25 pounds - through the air, into his left cheek, through his brain, and exited at the back of his skull.

You'd think that this type of accident would be fatal. Though Phineas survived. He lost his sight in his left eye and underwent both personality and intellectual changes. But despite having a pipe thrust right through the left side of his brain, he was able to remain working doing stable work for a while after the accident and then driving coaches in Chile before he settled down and passed away among family. Despite the enormous trauma and damage to his brain, he was able to continue living. [11]

Studies conducted on stroke patients have also shown how the brain is able to create new neural pathways to a different area in the brain when another area has become damaged. [12]

This is just how amazing your brain is. It is not a "fixed" organ, but capable of rewiring itself, establishing new connections, and adapting to change.

NEUROPLASTICITY VS NEUROGENESIS

These are two related, but different functions. Where neuroplasticity refers to the brain's ability to grow new connections and pathways in different areas of the brain, neurogenesis is the brain's ability to grow new neurons.

This is an extremely exciting concept as it means that we not only have the ability to change how our brains function, we're able to replace neurons that have died. Well, our brains are capable of doing that.

Most of your brain's neurons are already created by the time you are born. Before all these amazing new technological advancements, scientists believe that our brain cells die off a little at a time until the day we die. They never believed that we could grow new brain cells. But thanks to ongoing studies, scientists have been able to look at how new neurons are "born". Neurons (those billions of tiny messengers that carry messages all over the brain and body) form in areas of the brain where there are a lot of neural stem cells. Stem cell research is still in its infancy, but what they have observed to date is that stem cells have the ability to create new neurons and glial cells. Glial cells are like little bodyguards that support and protect the neurons.

This means that our brains are able to regenerate! How cool is that?

Okay, so what does all of this have to do with developing a growth mindset?

You now know that your brain is capable of change. This means that you are able to change your thoughts, your emotions, and your behaviors based on what you choose to focus on in your life. If you choose to focus on possibilities and practice building up certain skills, your brain will literally change itself to help you achieve what you want. On the flip side, if you choose to focus on all the negatives and what you perceive as your own shortcomings, your brain will support you in that too! You have to teach your brain what to focus on. You have to tend to the garden that is your mind and choose your thoughts very wisely. You have to put in the effort of practicing what you want to get better at.

Nothing in life comes easily, no matter what some TikTok videos might try to convey. You cannot just pick up a violin and play it if you've never practiced. Even if you're a type of savant (someone who is exceptionally and naturally talented and learned) you'd still need to practice to get better at something.

This means that with practice, and intentional focus, you can adopt a growth mindset. When you tap into that superpower within you, the sky's the limit when it comes to what you can achieve in your life.

Your brain is your ally, but you have to teach it what to do. Just like you had to teach yourself how to walk when you were a baby. You have to practice every single day and teach it what to focus on. As I said, it's ultimately your choice.

Either you choose to tap into your superpower, which is a growth mindset. Or you choose not to and go on to never fulfill your potential.

The choice is yours.

CHAPTER 3

6 COMMON GROWTH MINDSET ROADBLOCKS

"If you're trying to achieve, there will be roadblocks. I've had them; everybody has had them. But obstacles don't have to stop you. If you run into a wall, don't turn around and give up. Figure out how to climb it, go through it, or work around it." - Michael Jordan

No matter what you do or where you go in life, you will face obstacles. It's a natural part of life. It's how we learn. We face an obstacle, we adapt, we overcome. If you choose to.

Sometimes there are roadblocks that come our way that seem impossible to overcome. These usually have to do with our own thoughts and feelings. Those insecurities that we try to hide away from the rest of the world. Our deep-seated fears that we try our best not to show to anyone else.

You'll have to face these roadblocks head-on in order to overcome them. But first, you need to do some inner searching to find out what your personal roadblocks look like. Here are 6 of the most common roadblocks that most people face on their way to adopting a growth mindset.

1

A LACK OF CONFIDENCE

Confidence is one of those things that can either help us achieve amazing success, or keep us from living our dreams. It seems like some people are just born with it. Whether you are naturally inclined to have confidence in yourself or not has a lot to do with the kind of environment you grow up in. It's hard to lift yourself up when you live in an environment where people constantly try to break you down. Conversely, kids who grow up in a loving home where they are constantly lifted up by the grown-ups who surround them will have an easier time believing in themselves.

This is just one piece to the puzzle which is confidence. There are many other pieces. Like the way in which you speak to yourself. Your personality development. The friends that you surround yourself with, etc.

When you lack confidence it always goes hand-in-hand with a low sense of self-esteem. You may feel unloved or unlovable. You may feel incompetent, awkward, weird, or like you don't deserve to have confidence.

As human beings, we're pretty complex and there are so many factors that contribute to our sense of self. It's okay if you lack confidence. The important thing you need to know is that you can change it, even if it feels like you can't.

Here are some things you can try out to give your confidence a boost:

TURN YOUR FOCUS TO YOUR THOUGHTS.

- Pay some attention to the thoughts that tend to go through your mind on a daily basis. Are they telling you that you're capable or are they spewing lies like *"you're not good enough?"* Thoughts are just thoughts, they're not facts. Even so, it can be hard to shake negative thoughts even for those who are pros at tending to the garden that is their mind. Here's something you can try whenever you notice a negative thought pop into your head. It's very simple. Just add the word "yet" to whatever thought you're having. E.g. *"I'm not capable of doing this, YET."* This tells your mind that there is a possibility and helps it open up to more positivity.

- Ask yourself: "*Who am I trying to please?*" Because if you're only doing something to try and please someone else, let me tell you, it's a one-way ticket to unhappiness that will leave you with zero confidence.

- Make a list of things that you're good at. Sometimes we get so wrapped up focusing on the things we suck at, that we forget that there are things we're actually good at. Stick that list up somewhere where you can see it every day. Maybe on a wall in your room, on the fridge, on the bathroom mirror. Look at it every day and acknowledge your skills!

- Surround yourself with people who want the best for you. If your friends are not focused on getting better and wanting to do their best in life, find yourself some new friends. If you feel like there are certain words your parents use that make you feel like they think you're incapable, communicate that to them. Surround yourself with people who support you and push you to be the best version of yourself. Remember that study that showed that if you sit near someone who is a poor performer your performance will go down by 30%? Trust me, you do not want to make the mistake of surrounding yourself with the wrong people.

Having a growth mindset doesn't mean that you have confidence all the time. It means that you choose to focus on getting better by making yourself aware of your own blind spots and shortcomings. Then work on improving those areas in your life. That's what gives you confidence. Practice and experience.

Get out of your comfort zone. Join the debate team if you fear public speaking. Try out for the football team even if you have zero ball sense. Join music and singing classes even if you can't carry a tune. You get this one life to explore all of your capabilities. Try all of it out! This way you will eventually find what it is you love and can work on improving for the rest of your life.

2 FEAR OF FAILURE

I think we all struggle with this one at some point in our lives. The question is, why? When you're a baby you don't have that fear. When you're learning to walk you will fall many, many times. Though that doesn't stop you from trying because you fear failing again, does it? If that were the case none of us would ever learn to walk.

As we get older we learn to place value on other's opinions of ourselves. Meaning, that when someone laughs at you when you try something and fail, you remember that because it was embarrassing. Sometimes this keeps us from trying again. The weird thing is that we're only punishing ourselves. You're only withholding yourself from learning something new or developing a new skill. And more often than not, we make it into such a big deal inside of our heads, but once you've taken that step across the line that is your fear holding you back, you realize that it was actually not that big a deal.

HERE ARE SOME STRATEGIES TO HELP YOU OVERCOME YOUR FEAR OF FAILURE:

- Make a deal with yourself by committing yourself to your personal growth. Write up a contract if you have to. A promise you make to yourself to face your own fears and do what it takes to invest in your own growth in different areas of your life.

- Think of failure as a good thing. So many of us think of failure as a bad thing when it's actually an amazing gift. Yes, a gift! If we never made any mistakes or never failed at anything, we'd never learn. We learn *because* we make mistakes. Failure is just feedback provided to you on how not to do something. That's all it is. It's a good thing. Learn to embrace it.

- Feedback is your friend. I know I can sometimes be sensitive to feedback from other people. Feedback in the form of constructive criticism is a good thing. We all have blind spots and won't always be able to see what we're doing wrong. It can be very helpful when someone else can look at it from the outside and tell you what you're missing.

- What did you learn from your failures? Think back to a time when you failed at something. What did you learn from it? From now on, every night when you go to bed before you doze off, ask yourself: *"What did I learn today?"* Start priming your mind now to focus on lessons and growth, rather than on what it perceives as failure. It will serve you later on in life.

Failure is nothing other than an opportunity to do something differently. That's all you need to keep reminding yourself. *Failure = Opportunity.*

FEAR OF SUCCESS

3

Why on Earth would someone be afraid of success? I don't mean literally fearing success like: *"Oh no, please don't let me ever be successful!"* What I mean is that people often fear the consequences of success. Success usually comes with expectations from others. If you are a straight-A student, your parents and teachers might expect you to always be a straight-A student. Maybe you have 100K followers on TikTok and need to keep up with putting out content all the time. That puts a lot of pressure on you to perform.

HERE'S WHAT YOU CAN DO TO HELP YOURSELF GET OVER THIS KIND OF FEAR:

- Journaling. This is one of my favorite tools! You learn a lot about yourself through journaling. Ask yourself what it is you actually fear. Ask yourself the 5 Whys:

- What do I fear?
  Why do I fear it?
  Why is that?
  Why is that?
  Why is that?
  You ask yourself "Why is that" until you've gotten to the bottom of the issue.

- Remind yourself of your past successes. It's so easy for us to focus on our failures, but how often do you allow yourself to revel in your past successes? If you struggle to find something, write about positive things others have said about you. Maybe you got some positive feedback on a test recently? Or perhaps a teacher mentioned that you did something particularly well. Make a list of all the positive things you've been accomplishing of late.

- Focus on success. Where your attention goes, energy flows. If you're constantly thinking about the possibility of failing, chances are pretty good that you will fail. Sports professionals are taught how to focus on performing at the top of their game through visualizing it. Every morning, sit for a few minutes with your eyes closed and visualize your day. Visualize how you ace a test or how you score a goal at practice or at a game. You become what you choose to think about most of the time, so choose to see how you succeed so you can achieve it!

PERFECTIONISM

There is no such thing as perfect. So often we keep ourselves from achieving what we're actually capable of because we fear it not being perfect. I'm an overachiever, so trust me, I know what I'm talking about. I used to be sad when I scored anything under 90% on a test. I know. Boohoo. Poor me. The point I'm trying to make is that I caused myself to feel this sadness when I actually had no reason to do so. Unnecessary and self-inflicted punishment. That's what perfectionism is.

HERE'S HOW YOU CAN ADDRESS IT:

- Name it so you can tame it. We're circling back to journaling here. As I said, journaling is the best tool to help you get to know yourself better. When you're able to journal on a regular basis you'll start picking up on certain trends in your life that you may have not noticed before. It helps to get it out of your head and onto paper. Try to identify times when you have suffered from perfectionism. As you start to delve deeper into this tendency of yours, try to figure out where it comes from. What is causing it?

- Ask yourself this question: *"How is this helping you?"* Is it helping you? I mean does perfectionism really serve you in any way? Is there a downside to it? And if so, what does that look like?

- Start celebrating your small successes. Even if they're not perfect by your standards. Focus on embracing the things you do well, not perfect, but well.

- Remind yourself that failure is a gift, and to truly harness a growth mindset you need failure in your life. Failure is good. Failure is your friend. Failure is your teacher!

5

FEELING LIKE YOU'RE STUCK

This is another common obstacle many of us face. Especially when you don't know where you want to go or what you want to do with your life. How do you achieve something when you don't know what you want to achieve, right?

THIS MIGHT HELP YOU FIGURE IT OUT:

- Take some time out for self-reflection. Get back to that journal of yourself and explore what it is you like to do. What talents do you have? What interests you in life? Be curious about who you are and what you want.

- Brainstorm with a friend. Sometimes, when you're so stuck that you can't possibly see the way forward, a partner can help you figure it out. Someone else might be able to suggest things you've never even considered. Remember those blind spots we all have?

- You don't have to stick to something you don't like. Trying something out is great! Though if you find somewhere along the way that this just isn't for you, don't be afraid to change course. You can be whatever you want to be in life! So make sure that something is something you actually enjoy doing and are passionate about! There's no rule in life that says you HAVE to stick to one thing. Try out different things if you're feeling stuck. Experiment a little. Maybe you'll surprise yourself and discover an activity that you find enjoyable that you never even considered before

INERTIA

Inertia is basically that feeling that you get from not being able to move forward. A bit like being stuck. You find it difficult to get started on a project. You have tons of ideas but don't know where to start. You have an essay you need to write, but sit staring at your computer screen because you don't know what to do next.

KEY STEPS FOR TAKING ACTION:

- Break it down. Sometimes we struggle to start something because we feel overwhelmed. By breaking it down into smaller steps it might feel less intimidating and give you smaller, better-achievable goals.

- Create a schedule. You need dedicated work time and dedicated playtime. Structure your day according to your responsibilities, then figure out when you want to focus on the project and what you need to achieve during the time you've put aside for yourself. This way you know exactly what you need to focus on.

- Find an accountability partner who can help keep you on track by either checking in with you or working on the project together. Having someone who motivates you and makes sure you keep to your schedule might just be what you need to get the creative juices flowing.

- Set yourself multiple small goals throughout the day, then celebrate each small win you achieve. E.g. brushed my teeth this morning = win! Didn't kill my dufus brother = win! I'm kidding of course. But this helps to prime your brain to focus on the positives.

No matter the obstacle, there is always a solution. I'm a big believer in this. As the great Nelson Mandela said: "It always seems impossible until someone does it." Focus on solutions and you'll find what you're looking for. That's one of the main keys to developing a growth mindset. If you can think it, you can achieve it! [13]

EXERCISE

Fill out the form below, then come back to it on a weekly basis. You can copy it and stick it somewhere where you can see it. Update it on a constant basis.

List at least 5 things that you're good at:

Write down 3 lessons you've learned from failures in the past:

Write down at least 5 times you've succeeded at something in your life:

Write down 5 small successes you've had this week:

List 3 things you feel stuck on, then ask a friend for possible solutions:

Write down 3 goals you have for the next week:

CHAPTER 4

BEAT NEGATIVE SELF-TALK & LIMITING BELIEFS. DEVELOPING SELF-COMPASSION.

"The only thing limiting you is yourself." - Ken Poirot

HOW YOUR BELIEFS & SELF-TALK IMPACT YOUR REALITY

How often do you take note of the thoughts that run through your mind? When it comes to the things you think about yourself, how often do you take note of those? Are you aware of the way you address yourself in your mind? What about how you talk about yourself in front of others?

If you weren't aware of this before reading this book, the beliefs you hold about yourself and how you talk to yourself really matter a lot!

Are you kind to yourself inside your head? Or are you overly critical?

If you had to talk to your friends, the way you talk to yourself, how would they feel?

Your thoughts have such an impact on your life because they affect how you feel and how you act. If your self-talk is always negative, breaking yourself down, and being critical of yourself all the time, how do you expect that will make you feel? How do you think these feelings might impact your behavior?

If you can master your self-talk, you will be more confident, motivated, and productive in the long run.

A Japanese scientist named Dr. Masaru Emoto conducted experiments to see whether our thoughts have any effect on physical matter. One example I'd like to share with you is when he put water droplets under a microscope and photographed how the molecular structure of these water droplets changed based on the thoughts and emotions directed onto them.

When exposed to positive and loving thoughts and words like "thank you" and "I love you", the water crystals took on beautiful geometric shapes. When exposed to negative thoughts and words like "I hate you", the crystals morphed into more distorted shapes. Even music has an effect on matter. When exposed to heavy metal music, the water crystals would look like they were in pain almost. Completely devoid of any geometry or pattern. [14]

Now consider this: the human body comprises up to 60% water. Considering the factual evidence that these experiments have provided us with in terms of how our thoughts, words, and the things we expose ourselves to, like music, etc., we should really focus on how we talk to and about ourselves; and others!

Your thoughts and beliefs are so impactful that they can make you ill, they can heal you, they can even kill you. I know it sounds made up, but it's true.

Consider a little scientific phenomenon called the placebo effect.

Long ago there was a doctor who told people he could cure any disease they had by using metal pointers to "draw out" illness from the body. Of course, it was a total hoax, but what he found was unexpected. People actually got better. Some reported healing from diseases they had for a long time. The explanation? The placebo effect.

It's the same as when people are cured of certain ailments after being given a sugar pill in experiments and told that it's a certain medication.

What this teaches us is that our thoughts, and our beliefs, have great power!

This is why it's so important that you be careful about how you talk to and about yourself. Your thoughts and beliefs can have an exponential impact on your health, your performance, your success, your relationships, and every other perceivable aspect of your life. This is why it's so important that you tend the garden that is your mind. The way that you talk to yourself can have a considerable effect on your emotions and your behavior.

Negative self-talk has been shown to lead to higher levels of anxiety, depression, eating disorders, poor relationships, and poor performance in life. At its extreme, negative self-talk can even lead to suicidal tendencies. This is why it's so pertinent that we learn how to practice self-compassion and positive self-talk.

So how do you go about harnessing positive self-talk? Here are some tips for you to try out.

- **Start listening to your inner chatter:** Pay attention to your thoughts for a few days. Write them down in your journal and try to identify your negative self-talk patterns. Awareness is always the first step toward change. Make a list of all the negative things you tell yourself like: "I suck" "I'm such a loser" or "Nobody loves me."

- **Examine the evidence:** Are these statements you tell yourself really true? Are they helpful? Are they serving you in any way? Are they facts, or just thoughts? Are you being unfair toward yourself? Where is this coming from? What is causing this?

- **Focus on what you're grateful for:** When your mind is filled with negative beliefs about yourself it can be hard to just shift gears and suddenly focus on positive self-talk. Start by focusing on the things you're grateful for in your life. It can be something small like your pet, or the fact that you can breathe. This will help in priming your mind to shift its focus to focus on more positive thoughts.

- **Take a step back:** When you're stuck in a loop of negative thinking it can be extremely challenging to try and see yourself from a different perspective. Try to take a step back and ask yourself: "Would I talk to my best friend this way?" Would you tell your best friend that they are the things you believe about yourself? E.g. "You're useless." Don't you think they'd feel hurt if you spoke to them like that? Ask yourself why you would address yourself in that manner.

- **Lean on your support system:** That's what a support system is there for. When you're really struggling, reach out and talk to someone you trust. Ask your parents to see a therapist so they can help you work through your negative beliefs. A professional can also help you come up with strategies on how to challenge these beliefs going forward.

- **Box it:** If you feel overwhelmed and unable to challenge your negative thoughts/beliefs, box them. Put them away in a box for later when you feel more up to the task. You can take it back out when you're journaling or maybe when you go to see your therapist so they can help you work through what you're struggling with. [15]

OUR BRAINS JUMP TO CONCLUSIONS

Jumping to conclusions is something many of us struggle with. You see your best friend with that girl you like so much and immediately think to yourself: "I can't believe he would betray me like that!" You made a split-second decision on what was going on based on very little information. All you actually know is that your best friend is talking to the girl that you like. Though, when we struggle with negative self-chatter, our brains also often go to the first negative explanation that comes up. The problem is, these assumptions are wrong more often than not and can easily wreck a relationship.

Jumping to conclusions is a type of negative thought pattern that psychologists refer to as "cognitive distortions". These are basically faulty ways of thinking. Many people who suffer from negative thought patterns also suffer from cognitive distortions. This often leads to experiencing symptoms of anxiety and depression. It makes sense, right? If you're constantly stuck focusing on the negative and on everything that could go wrong, that would cause anyone to feel depressed.

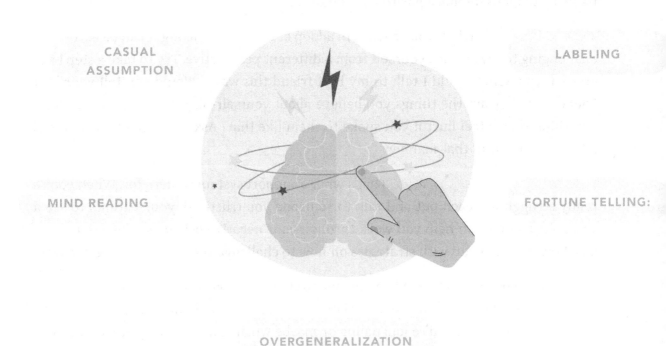

CASUAL
ASSUMPTION

LABELING

MIND READING

FORTUNE TELLING:

OVERGENERALIZATION

Here are a few examples of how people tend to jump to conclusions:

- Casual Assumption: This is when people immediately make an assumption based on what they see. Like in the example above. Another example might be when you assume that a friend is angry at you because they haven't spoken to you all day. In reality, they're struggling with something that happened at home. You made an assumption based on very little information without asking your friend outright if they're angry with you. Your assumption was wrong, which might lead to you avoiding your friend, which leads them to think that you're angry with them. See how it can blow up?

- Mind Reading: Although we might want to believe ourselves to be good at reading other people's minds, we're actually quite bad at it. This, again, refers to you making an assumption based on very little information. E.g. you greet a friend as you walk past them but they don't greet you back. In your mind, you're thinking that they are upset with you when in reality, they just didn't hear you. You assumed to know what was going through their mind.

- Overgeneralization: This is a type of cognitive distortion that results in you thinking that because you had one bad experience related to a single incident, you will always have that bad experience. For example, a teacher who reprimands you in class for not having done your homework. This was one incident but in your mind, you think: "Teachers *always* give me a hard time." "I can't do anything right." Which isn't true of course as it was just one incident.

- Fortune Telling: This one is a bit like jumping to conclusions, except that in this case it relates to predicting what will happen in the future. It usually relates to negative beliefs you hold about yourself. E.g. "I am going to do badly on this test next week." It's something that's happening next week. You still have time to study. Yet your thoughts go straight to that negative place of telling yourself that you're going to fail.

- Labeling: This one has to do with making an assumption about a group of people, based on one person's behavior or assumptions you make about that one person. An example would be assuming that only boys like to play video games. This isn't true of course, but maybe you just haven't met girls who like to play video games and made that assumption. Another example might be that a blonde boy bullied you, so now you think all blonde boys are bullies. Again, this isn't true of course but you take the behavior of one person and apply it to a certain group.

Jumping to conclusions often results in causing conflicts in your relationships with the people in your life. This can range from your friends to your teachers and parents. If you are constantly jumping to conclusions about other people it can lead to misunderstandings and arguments that are unnecessary to begin with.

It can also have a negative effect on how you think about yourself. If you constantly believe that the people around you are being mean to you, cheating on you, angry with you, etc. what does that say about you? Eventually, you start telling yourself things like "I am unlovable" "Nobody loves me" "Nobody wants to be my friend" and "Nobody cares about me." Do you see how that can have a detrimental effect on your life? This type of thinking and beliefs often lead to teens experiencing great levels of anxiety and depression, and even suicidal ideation. And so often, it was just a misunderstanding.

I'm sure you are now able to see how important it is that you take some time to investigate before jumping to a conclusion. How do you do that though? Here are some strategies for you to try out:

- Fact or fiction?: When you notice yourself forming a belief based on little information ask yourself: "Is this a fact or just a thought?" Challenge that thought by asking for more information. That friend who didn't greet you back? Ask them if something's bothering them or why they didn't greet you back.

- Another explanation: Ask yourself whether there might be another explanation for what you observed. E.g. your friend just didn't hear you when you greeted them and that's why they didn't greet you back.

- A different perspective: Try just looking at the problem from a different point of view. If you were someone else, how might they interpret the situation? [16]

EXERCISE

Think of a time when you jumped to a conclusion and were wrong. What happened and how could you have approached it differently using the above examples?

_____

_____

_____

_____

_____

_____

_____

_____

_____

_____

_____

_____

_____

_____

_____

_____

_____

_____

Beat Negative Self-Talk & Limiting Beliefs. Developing Self-Compassion.

45

DEVELOPING A CAN-DO ATTITUDE

A negative attitude will almost certainly drag you down in life. Can you think of someone who is successful and has a negative attitude? Neither can I. It just doesn't work that way. As the famous self-development expert Tony Robbins has said time and again *"Where your focus goes, energy flows."* It's as simple as that. If you keep thinking that you're going to fail, you shouldn't be surprised when you do. [17]

You have a choice in life. Either you choose to take on a growth mindset and make things happen for yourself, or, you can simply shrug your shoulders and give up by adopting a fixed mindset.

Though just think of all the possibilities if you choose to take control of your life and go after your dreams! Imagine those dreams coming true. How amazing would that be? Isn't it far more exciting and worth your time to put all that you have into sculpting the life you truly want? I think so.

The most exciting fact is that you can change your mindset. You can harness positive thoughts over time. You can make a habit of living a happy life.

Here are 6 ways to help you on your way:

1. START WITH YOUR MINDSET.

We already know that we need to develop a growth mindset. Your mindset really is the foundation of all things to follow in your life. Put in the time and effort to develop such a strong mindset that no matter what anyone says, you will always believe in yourself. You don't need others' approval. You can achieve whatever you set out for yourself! Do you know how many times people have told top athletes and famous businesspeople they'd fail? Did they listen to those people? No. Imagine if they did. We'd have no Mike Tyson, Albert Einstein, Muhammad Ali, Michael Jordan, etc.

2. THE THREE-LEGGED STOOL

Although your thoughts and the type of things you focus on are extremely important, they alone will not change your life. You can think of all the positive thoughts in the world, but unless you do something about it, nothing will happen. It's like that story where a man is stuck on an island and prays to God to save him. A ship appears and tries to save the man, but he replies: "No thank you. God will save me." He prays to God again to save him. Another ship arrives, but the man again refuses to get on board saying: "No thank you, God will save me." This happens a third time, after which a massive cyclone engulfs the tiny island and the man with it. When the man gets to heaven he asks God, "Why didn't you save me?" To which God replies, I sent you three ships but you refused to get on.

In the same way, you can have all the positive thoughts and life can present you with all the opportunities, but unless you act in accordance with what you want you'll end up stuck forever.

Your thoughts, feelings, and actions are interlinked. If you think positive thoughts but feel negative feelings, how will you behave? Each of these is one of the legs of your three-legged stool. If you don't want it to fall over you need to give equal amounts of care and attention to each of the three constituents. Your thoughts, your feelings, and your actions. How do you do that?

• *Align your thoughts with your actions.*

Start focusing on what you can do instead of what you can't. You can put in the effort to work on your weaknesses so you can get better at doing hard things. You can also focus on your strengths and achieve as much as you can with the talents that you have.

• *How you ACT impacts how you FEEL.*

It doesn't help if you focus on positive, reaffirming thoughts about your abilities today and then give up and tell yourself you're not capable tomorrow. You need to act in accordance with what you want to feel. Want to feel like a success? Then act like someone who is successful. Someone who is successful works hard in life. They do their chores. They do their homework. They work on both their strengths and weaknesses every single day.

• *Use how you FEEL to reinforce the way you THINK.*

The way you feel has a big impact on how you present yourself to the world and ultimately think of yourself. Are you slouching or hunched forward in your seat? Sit up straight! Have you ever seen how characters in TV shows or films use the superhero pose to help boost their confidence? There's a science to it. Your posture, the way you walk, and the expression on your face impacts how you feel.

3. BE MINDFUL OF YOUR SELF-TALK

Your self-worth is directly linked to your self-talk. Sometimes our self-talk is based on how the adults in our lives treat us. A successful basketball player once visited a prison to work with inmates on helping them harness more positive mindsets and focus on how they can do better when they'd get out of prison. He told them how, when he was a little boy his dad used to say to him: "My son, if you keep dunking balls like that you'll end up an NBA player." And he did.

One of the inmates responded by saying: "My dad used to say things to me as well growing up. He used to always focus on the things I did wrong and say:" If you keep doing stuff like that you'll end up in prison one day." And he did.

How the people around us treat us can have a great impact on the foundation from which we operate later in life. Though what you need to teach yourself and understand now whilst you're still young is that YOU get to decide what you CHOOSE to FOCUS on. It's easier said than done. But just remember that NOBODY can break you down if you choose to believe in yourself. If you put in the work day in and day out to become a success. Only YOU have that power.

So be mindful of what you repeatedly tell yourself in your head and the thoughts you choose to focus on. I know I sound like a parrot repeating myself, but I can't stress enough just how important this point is.

4. BE ACTIVE, NOT PASSIVE.

Being active means you harness positive thoughts and ideas, and then you act on them. You go out and make it happen. Being passive means you might harness those positive thoughts and ideas, but then you sit like the guy on that island and don't do anything about it. What do you think is going to happen if you don't do anything about it? Nothing. Or life will just take you wherever it wants to. Take up the driver's seat rather than being a passenger in your own car that is your life.

Be mindful of opportunities and take them when they come along.

5. ACCEPT AND LEARN FROM YOUR MISTAKES.

Start seeing mistakes as learning opportunities rather than failures. Remember, mistakes are just feedback given to us on how not to do something. It offers us valuable information on what we need to change to do better. Mistakes are your friend. Start embracing it. Learn from it.

6. CHANGE YOUR LOCUS OF CONTROL.

The what? Locus of control basically means that you either place your own value on what people outside of you say, or what you believe on the inside. Do you position the power of your experiences inside or outside of yourself? Do you give power to others or to yourself? If your locus of control is outside of yourself, it means that others have the power to affect how you feel. When your locus of control is internal, only you have the power to dictate what you think, and how you feel and behave.

Developing your attitude to be more focused on possibilities and positives is maybe one of the best gifts you can give yourself. Your attitude almost always predicts your altitude, or how far you will go in life. So it's worth putting in the time and effort now to build a solid foundation for when you're older. [18]

EXERCISE

Write down 6 statements that begin with "I am…" followed by a positive trait that you possess. For example: "I am smart. I am good at sports. I am a good student."

Then, write down 6 things you hope to be someday, but write it in the present tense like you did the first 6, e.g. "I am a successful businesswoman. I have the house of my dreams. I am a professional football player."

In the now:

_____

_____

_____

_____

In the future: (but in the present tense)

_____

_____

_____

_____

_____

"We are our own harshest critics." Maybe you've heard someone say that before. It gets said a lot because, well, it's true. Maybe there are people in your life who are hard on you. But I'm betting you're even harder on yourself, right?

What's even more unfair is that we're often hard on ourselves for not succeeding at something when - we have in fact - never been taught *how* to do what we aim to succeed at. Has anyone ever taught you about self-compassion and about how important it is that you be kind to yourself in the way that you speak to yourself in your mind? No? Then you can't blame yourself for not knowing how to do it in the first place.

Self-compassion basically means giving yourself a break for not being perfect and not getting everything right the first time around. It's reminding yourself that you're only human and that you will make mistakes, and that's okay. In fact, as you know by now, I'm in favor of mistakes.

Having self-compassion means you regard yourself in a positive way and treat yourself with love and care. You treat yourself the way you want others to treat you.

The practice of self-compassion also bears close ties with the practice of mindfulness. Mindfulness is what allows us to be aware of what's going on in and outside of us in the present moment. This can help you pick up on when you're being overly harsh with yourself and need to adjust your attitude.

Having compassion for yourself is really no different from having compassion for others. Here are a few examples of how you can start to practice self-compassion:

1. SPEAK TO YOURSELF AS YOU WOULD A FRIEND

We've briefly touched on this before. It's an easy way of reminding yourself to practice self-compassion. If you're a good friend you'd want what's best for your friends. When they come to you feeling like they've failed, you'll probably talk them up and say something like: "Hey, don't worry about it. You'll do better next time. This isn't the end of the world. Your mistakes don't define you." Aim to speak to yourself the same way. With a warm, soft, compassionate tone.

2. BECOME MORE SELF-AWARE

This ties in with practicing mindfulness. By taking some time out on a daily basis to tap into what's going on inside of us, we can become aware of thoughts and feelings that do not serve us and need changing. We sometimes don't even realize when we've been talking to ourselves in a harsh or critical way until we take a moment to think about our day or what is going on inside of us. Journaling is another way of becoming more aware of your own inner critic. Journaling on a regular basis will help you identify patterns relating to your self-talk.

3. YOU'RE NOT ALONE

Although you might feel like you're the only one who has to struggle with the thoughts and feelings that you do, I can guarantee you that you're not. We all experience negative self-talk and we are all our own harshest critics. Talk to a friend and tell them how you've been feeling. I can almost promise you that they might say they've struggled with something similar. Knowing that you're not the only one in the world who struggles with negative self-talk can help you not place so much weight on it, and in turn, practice more self-compassion.

The world is already harsh enough without you needing to be harsh with yourself as well. You don't need to be. The purpose of this life isn't to be perfect and never make mistakes. It's about learning, failing, getting back up, learning more, failing again, getting back up, etc. It's a journey! So go easy on yourself. You've got this! [19]

RECOGNIZING MEAN THOUGHTS ABOUT YOURSELF

Sometimes we attach a belief to a feeling because we don't know any better. Emotions are powerful things that can have a very positive or very negative impact on our lives. The question is whether you're aware of what you allow yourself to focus on. Let's do a little exercise to help you both recognize and overcome negative or mean thoughts or beliefs about yourself.

REPLACE "I AM" WITH "I FEEL."

E.g. I am broken = I *FEEL* broken. (What you feel is not what you are and this exercise will help you identify the feelings that you mistake for "truths" about who you are.

_____

_____

_____

_____

REPLACE OLD TRUTHS WITH NEW ONES.

Now take the new beliefs you've written down above that start with "I feel" and rewrite them using this example: **"I feel not good enough"** = **"I am good enough. I am just having a hard time with this project because it entails a lot of math that I am not yet good at."** The words "not yet" are very important here as it signals something that is yet to happen. So just because you might not be good at certain aspects of math now, doesn't mean you won't get better at it.

_____

_____

_____

_____

Once you've completed this exercise, take your new beliefs and do something constructive with it. E.g. take an extra math class after school. Look up Youtube lessons on how to draw if what you want to get better at is sketching. Sign up for a free coding course. There are so many resources available to you today on the internet. Many of them are for free. Take advantage of that to learn and grow as much as you possibly can. You'll thank yourself later in life. Trust me. [20]

REPLACE	FOR
I am not good enough. I am a failure. I am a loser. I am incompetent. Everyone is better than me. I will never succeed.	I am worthy. I am constantly learning to become better and do my best to do so.
I am bad. I don't deserve anything. Everything I do is wrong.	I am good. I can be good. I want to be good. I do what's right and try to fix it when I don't. I am learning to be better.
I am ugly. I am undesirable. I am unlovable. I am unattractive.	I am deserving of love. I am beautiful just as I am. I love myself and so do others.
Everything is my fault. I never get anything right.	I sometimes get things right. I choose to see failures as opportunities to learn and grow.
People cannot be trusted. People are mean. I can't get close to anyone.	Some people can be trusted. Not everyone is out to hurt me. There are people who have shown me love and kindness.
There is no point in life. Life is unfair. Life is not worth living.	Life is a gift if I choose to see it as such. Life is full of possibilities. Life is worth living.

HOW TO ESTABLISH HEALTHY BOUNDARIES

This is an extremely important issue in life. If you are able to learn how to effectively set boundaries with others early on in life, it will make dealing with relationships so much easier as you get older.

We often struggle to set boundaries with others, especially the people we are close with because we do not want to upset them or make them feel offended. The thing is, you have to teach people how you want them to treat you. Otherwise, there will always be someone who tries to maybe take advantage of you or see how much they can get out of you.

This relates to both your friends and the adults in your life. You have a right to say no to certain things in life. Especially when it comes to things that people do that make you feel uncomfortable. You have to learn how to protect yourself and the relationships you will enter into. The way you do that is through clear communication and healthy boundaries.

There are 5 different types of boundaries. The 5th boundary, which is financial, might not be very relatable to you right now, but it's good to learn about it early on so you have this knowledge in the bank for later on.

1. Physical Boundaries:

This type of boundary relates to your physical body and your personal space. Some of us don't like it when others touch us, even if it's just a friend jokingly punching our shoulder. Others are more comfortable with holding hands with a boyfriend/girlfriend, but not with anyone else. I, for example, do not like it when people stand too close to me.

2. Sexual Boundaries:

This is another important one for both boys and girls. No one has the right to touch you in an intimate manner. NO ONE! You have every right to say no and should tell someone if someone has forced you to touch them or be touched when you didn't want to.

3. Intellectual Boundaries:

You have a right to your own beliefs and opinions. This boundary relates more to people who do not respect your beliefs or opinions like your choice of religion or political beliefs. Everyone is different and everyone is allowed to have their own beliefs. Just as you cannot tell someone else what they should believe, they also cannot tell you.

4. Emotional Boundaries:

This boundary relates to your feelings. Sometimes people will try and force you to share with them what you're feeling. This is not okay and you have a right to say no. Just as people need to respect your right to hold your own beliefs, the same applies to your feelings.

5. Financial Boundaries:

This one is all about money and might not relate to you as much at the moment. Though, even when it comes to pocket money or wages you earn from a weekend job, you can do with that money whatever you want. It's yours. So if a friend asks you to buy them something or asks you for a loan, you have a right to say no without needing to feel bad about it.

Setting boundaries is a way of protecting yourself in different aspects of your life. People who do not set boundaries with both themselves and others usually end up in unhappy relationships or friendships. On that point, setting boundaries with yourself is just as important. Without it, you will struggle with self-discipline and sticking to your values.

You need to set boundaries with yourself in terms of the type of person you choose to be. The things you choose to want to achieve. The things you choose to believe are important in life. For example, I choose to always be honest and tell the truth no matter what. That's a boundary you set with yourself. "I choose to do my homework every day and try to turn my Cs into Bs this year by taking extra classes." That's a boundary you set with yourself.

Okay but how about setting boundaries with other people? How do we do that? Consider the following steps:

Why do you want to set this boundary?

You need to have an understanding of why this boundary is important to you so you can communicate that reason more clearly to someone else. If you don't understand why this is important, how do you expect someone else to understand it?

Start small.

It can be a bit of a shock to the system if you've never set boundaries with your friends and now all of a sudden you're saying no to everything. They won't understand. You also wouldn't understand if someone did that to you. So start small with one or two boundaries at first. You can always build up to more.

Early on is easier.

It's always easier to set boundaries with someone new. When you're into a 5-year long relationship it can be hard to change things up all of a sudden. So when you meet someone new and they do something that makes you uncomfortable, set a boundary there and then, communicate why you don't like what they just did and that you'd appreciate it if they didn't do it again.

Consistency is key.

What's even more important than setting a boundary is enforcing that boundary. I can guarantee you that there will be people who will try and push your boundaries. Not everyone will do it on purpose. Some people just need reminding of a new boundary more than once. However, if someone keeps disrespecting your boundaries it's usually best to remove them from your life by not being friends anymore.

Take time out for yourself.

In some families, there's little to no time for yourself because you may have multiple siblings or a busy household. It's important to take some quality time for yourself from time to time to reflect on your week, how you're feeling, and what your goals are, or doing something you enjoy like painting or whatever it is. Tell your parents when you need some alone time and ask them to not interrupt you. The same goes for your friends.

Set healthy boundaries on social media.

A boundary in real life is also a boundary on the internet. If a friend crosses your boundary on social media it's still crossing a boundary. E.g. Let's say a friend teases you on social media about something that you believe but they don't. They know not to do this to your face because you've set that boundary. You need to remind them that it is a boundary in all realms. Online, offline, other dimensions, it doesn't matter.

It's also a good idea to set boundaries with yourself regarding who you follow and who you allow to follow you on social media. Getting millions of followers is no big deal nowadays. Having a million followers doesn't mean that someone's an awesome person. Maybe they're just posing as someone who's a good person but later starts teaching people to hate themselves. You don't need that kind of influence in your life. Be very careful and picky about who you allow to have access to you and your attention in your life. Both on and offline.

You've crossed a boundary.

It's important that you communicate with someone when they've crossed one of your boundaries. As I've said, not everyone will do this out of spite or to test you. Some people just need reminding as it's something new and they just didn't realize that they've crossed a boundary. Always tell someone when they've crossed one of your boundaries.

It can feel really uncomfortable to set boundaries at first. I promise you that it gets better with time. I used to be someone who could never set boundaries with others because I was so scared they wouldn't like me anymore or that they would feel offended or hurt. Now that I know how to set boundaries, I practice it on a regular basis.

My relationships with friends and family have never been better. That also goes with my relationship with myself because this act of setting boundaries has taught me that I'm deserving of respect. Boundaries are how I respect myself.

Once you're more aware of your own boundaries it's also important that you honor the boundaries of others. When a friend communicates a boundary of theirs with you, make sure to respect that.

Besides, you would want the same from them, right?

Fill out this assessment to see where you're at on the self-love scale. This will give you a good idea of which areas you might need to pay extra attention to.

SELF-LOVE ASSESSMENT

Once you've completed this assessment it will give you something to come back to in the future to measure how much you've grown, and which areas still need more work.

0 = Never   2 = Sometimes   4 = Most of the time

1 = Rarely   3 = Frequently   5 = Always

1. I believe I am good enough and valuable

0   1   2   3   4   5

2. It is okay for me to make mistakes and not be perfect.

0   1   2   3   4   5

3. I can communicate what I want and need with ease.

0   1   2   3   4   5

4. I know when I am struggling and know how to support myself in those times.

0   1   2   3   4   5

5. I believe I am worthy and deserving of love.

0   1   2   3   4   5

6. I accept and love my body just as it is.

0   1   2   3   4   5

7. I know my abilities and strengths and how to use them when I face challenges.

0   1   2   3   4   5

8. My feelings are just as important as everyone else's.

0   1   2   3   4   5

9. I do not need a romantic relationship or validation from my friends to feel good about myself.

0   1   2   3   4   5

10. I make a point to take care of myself and do nice things for myself.

0   1   2   3   4   5

SCORE:

40 - 50: You are a self-love rockstar and have a strong ability to love yourself. Keep doing what you're doing!

30 - 39: You have a strong foundation of self-love. Keep investing in different ways to develop your self-love abilities. Practice regularly.

20 - 29: There are days when you feel good about yourself, but then there are days when you struggle with self-love. The more you invest in yourself, the more good days you will have. Keep practicing!

10 - 19: Loving yourself completely is a challenge for you. You are capable of learning your own value, you just need to invest more time and effort in activities to help you build on the foundation that you already have. You can do it!

0 - 9: You're new to the self-love game. That's okay. You are strong, capable, and ready to start! Take some time out of your schedule on a weekly basis to focus on just yourself. Work through the exercises in this book, and look up different self-love exercises online that you can use to help boost your self-love game.

SELF-REFLECTION:

Based on your score above, reflect on areas you think you can improve on and what you can do to boost your own self-love game.

_____

_____

_____

_____

_____

_____

_____

_____

_____

_____

_____

_____

_____

_____

_____

_____

_____

_____

CHAPTER 5

DEALING WITH SETBACKS & FAILURES.

"Success is not final, failure is not fatal: it is the courage to continue that counts."— Winston S. Churchill

HOW SOMEONE WITH A GROWTH MIND-SET VIEW THEIR MISTAKES

Let's face it, none of us *like* to make mistakes. The reality is that you *will* make mistakes. It's just a part of life. Even if we don't like it.

Why don't we naturally feel so bad when we make mistakes? Have you ever thought of that? When we are babies, going through our toddler years, we make many mistakes on a daily basis. Stumbling and falling when we try to walk. Spitting up food when we should be swallowing. Putting things in our mouths that are not meant for eating. We don't think to ourselves: "Man I'm such a bad baby. I can't even swallow my pureed pumpkin the way I should."

As we get older we start creating and becoming more aware of this thing we call an "ego". We now start to feel embarrassed when we make mistakes and our *"ego gets bruised."* We become more aware of ourselves and what we think others think of us. We want others to like us, especially the people close to us like our friends and our teachers. Our parents have to like us, they have no choice. I'm kidding. We of course want to impress our parents and have them be proud of us.

The strange thing is, even though we know that we need to make mistakes to learn, we still feel bad when we make them. Making a mistake in the classroom will leave you feeling embarrassed. Failing in front of your parents might leave you feeling like a failure.

Imagine if everyone just gave up because they experienced failure or made mistakes. We'd be extinct by now.

What makes us uniquely human is the fact that we have this big bulbous brain that allows us to learn from our mistakes so we can improve and do better.

When you start to embrace a growth mindset, you come to learn that mistakes are your friend. Teens who choose to adopt and nurture a growth mindset view their mistakes as opportunities to expand their knowledge base and learn new things. There is no end in sight. We never stop learning. The only constant in our lives, until the day we die, is change. Every single day there is so much change happening around you both on a molecular and macro scale.

Someone who has a growth mindset is continually focusing their attention on improving themselves. Improving their knowledge. Improving their skills. Improving their health. Improving their relationships. They focus on improving every aspect of their lives.

People are often looking for the "easy" or "quick" way. Anything just to not have to put in too much effort. Let me tell you a little secret. There are no shortcuts. There's no such thing as getting rich quickly unless you miraculously win the lottery. Even gamers have to put in thousands of hours to make the money they do.

This doesn't mean you have to work yourself to death and barely have a life. What I'm trying to point out is that having a growth mindset will help you find ways of working *smart, and* finding solutions that others might not have thought of before because they're still stuck in a fixed mindset. The world is changing all the time. Just take the Covid-19 pandemic for example. So many people lost their jobs, their families, their homes. Who's to say something like that won't happen in our lifetime again? And if it does, will you be the kind of person who has used his/her opportunities to learn from mistakes wisely?

Remember what I said to you earlier in this book? Mistakes and failures are nothing more than feedback provided to you on how not to do something. That feedback is very valuable as it shows you where not to go. If you don't listen to that feedback, you'll keep ending up in the wrong place in your life.

Learn to listen to the wisdom of your mistakes. Listen very carefully. Every aspect of your life can be improved with constant effort and improved knowledge and skills. Don't fall into the trap of thinking you do not have control over your destiny. Because you do. [21]

ACKNOWLEDGE AND EMBRACE IMPERFECTION

We live in the age of technology. That means that you have all the information in the world available to you, right at your fingertips. It also means that millions of companies around the world are bidding to have their products, services, and ads seen by the masses. Social media paints pictures of idyllic lives, perfect families, and smoking-hot bodies. We are constantly comparing ourselves with what we see on our screens.

In reality, everyone is imperfect. Even the people we idolize. No one person on this planet is perfect. Not even your crush. Even if you may think so right now.

There's a lot of pressure out there for us to be perfect. To have the perfect hairstyle. To wear the perfect clothes. Go on the perfect holiday. Eat the perfect food. Take the perfect photos and videos to show your followers on TikTok that you're perfect. You're not. Neither are they.

All this pressure for perfection is constantly chipping away at our self-esteem, making us feel like we will never be enough.

This is how illness is born.

You are perfectly imperfect.

I know it's hard to believe that right now. Believe me when I say that as you get older, you start to learn that nothing you thought was crucial in your teens ends up being important in your 20s, 30s, or 40s. It's like we live back-to-front. It seems that it's only later in life that we start to really accept ourselves for who we are. If you're lucky anyway. Most people never get there because they forever feel like they need to keep up with the Joneses, the Kardashians, or whichever famous family comes next.

Even though we are all imperfect, you are perfect in your own unique way. I know that sounds like a paradox. But no one else can be you.

As the great Dr. Seuss would say: "*Today you are You, that is truer than true. There is no one alive who is Youer than you.*" [22]

Do you know what the odds are of you being born? About 1 in 400 trillion! Those are almost impossible odds. Yet here you are. Reading this book. You were meant to be here, now, on this planet, living this life, having this human experience. So even if you're not perfect, you're pretty special.

I know you're under a lot of pressure to be interesting, beautiful, funny, rich, and perfect. But please hear me today: if your focus is on perfection, you will never be happy.

Instead, focus on embracing your own imperfections.

When you do that, you give yourself permission to chase after your biggest goals and dreams without having a specific outcome in mind. When it doesn't have to be perfect it means you can make mistakes, learn, and improve along the way. It means that you might even arrive at an even better destination than you set out for.

Embracing imperfection feels like:

Using mistakes you make along the way as part of the learning process.

Having the freedom to chase after the goals that you want to achieve for yourself.

You're able to recognize and celebrate your strengths and accomplishments.

Knowing that, no matter what, you are a person worthy of love and respect, regardless of your success, mistakes, or position in life.

Accepting that even if you haven't achieved your goals quite yet, you can enjoy the journey and where you are right now in your life.

EMBRACING YOUR IMPERFECTIONS = FREEDOM.

When you are chasing perfection, you enslave yourself to the latest trends around the world. I guarantee you 100% that you will never be able to keep up with what the world thinks is perfect. You don't want to do that, trust me. It's not worth it. [23]

You're worthy of being perfectly imperfect. Learn to be kind to yourself and to love yourself.

Learn to let go.

TREAT CHALLENGES AS OPPORTUNITIES FOR GROWTH

Your comfort zone is where dreams go to die.

You will have to face many different challenges in your life. You'll also have to choose which you want to take on and which you don't. Furthermore, you also get to choose how you treat challenges in general.

Someone with a fixed mindset would shy away from challenges. They'd want to find a comfortable job doing something they're relatively good at, where they have security and very little in the way of obstacles or challenges. Does that sound like an environment that will help you grow as a person? No.

Taking on a new challenge can certainly be frightening as we always face the possibility of failure. Though it also presents us with an opportunity to learn more about ourselves.

I once took on a massive challenge in my life. Something that people thought wasn't possible. It was so big a challenge that even I had my doubts. But you know what, I learned so much about myself along the way. I learned a whole lot about people and life in general as well. I chose to see every obstacle that came my way as an opportunity to learn. And in the end, I succeeded in completing what I set out to do. I would not be the person I am today if it was not for that major challenge in my life.

How many times have you heard successful and famous athletes, businessmen and women, adventurers, and multi-million dollar influencers tell a story about a challenge they faced in their life that they had to overcome and how it made them the person they are today? Nothing worthy comes easily, and nothing that comes easy is ever really worth it.

There are of course times when we need to be realistic about certain challenges. Especially the kind of challenge that can put our lives in danger, or the kind of challenge that has a 99.9%

chance of seeing you fail. You obviously need to be smart about which challenges you choose to take on. If it's going to hurt you or someone else, it's obviously not something worth considering.

What I'm referring to is more related to facing up to a challenge that's worth taking, instead of making up excuses. This applies to everyday challenges as well. It can be a challenge to get up early and work out if that's a goal of yours. Will you take up the challenge or do you make up excuses as to why you've missed the 154th morning in a row? Maybe you're aiming at improving your marks at school. Are you facing up to the challenge of putting in the extra work, or do you retreat to your comfort zone and watch TV the whole day?

Challenges come in all kinds of shapes and sizes. You get big challenges and small challenges. Short challenges and long challenges. Semi-easy challenges and difficult challenges.

If you want to live an authentic and fulfilling life, you need to do things that challenge you as an individual. How will you ever know who you truly are if you don't try out different things? There are many successful people out there who didn't take on certain challenges earlier on in their lives because they feared failing. It's never too late, but it's so much easier when you start out with a growth mindset early on in life. That's what smart people do. They learn from those who came before us. Learn what works, and doesn't. Trying to avoid challenges does not work, trust me. Try out different things. Be prepared to fail. Also, be prepared to grow.

Fear cannot hurt you if you choose to befriend it.

BE RECEPTIVE TO FEEDBACK & OPEN TO SELF-IMPROVEMENT

Feedback is the fuel that drives personal development. I know it can sometimes feel like someone's picking on you or telling you that you're not good enough when they give you feedback. As long as it's constructive and aimed at helping you get better at something, it's a good thing.

It's one of the core values of a growth mindset. Anyone who aims to be the best at something or the most successful at something knows that feedback is what helps them improve.

I used to be an off-road motorcycle instructor and feedback was the number one thing that helped my students improve. As someone standing on the outside, I could easily pick up on what they were doing that led them to not be able to complete an exercise. Maybe their body position was not quite where it should be, or they were looking in the wrong place, not controlling the throttle as they should. By providing them with constructive feedback along with instructions on how to improve, they were able to adjust what they were doing and get better at controlling their bike through a particular exercise.

This is just a simple example. Like I've said before, we all have blind spots and it helps to have someone on the outside give us feedback on what we need to change to do better.

When you finish school you'll want to pursue some kind of career. Whether it's as a lawyer, an astronaut, a doctor, a YouTuber, a singer, or a gamer, it doesn't matter. For you to get better at what you're doing, you'll need feedback. This might be a manager or a boss giving you feedback on areas they want to see you improving in. As a YouTuber, your channel statistics will give you invaluable feedback on your performance and areas you need to improve upon. As an astronaut, your trainers and superiors will constantly be giving you feedback on what they see you're doing and what you need to change. As an entrepreneur, your profit margin will give you feedback on how well your business is doing.

It's up to you how you choose to receive the feedback you are guaranteed to receive.

Here are 5 tips on how to be more receptive to feedback.

1. **Take some time to think about the feedback you've received and its potential value.**

Although we're prone to be emotionally reactive to feedback, don't be too quick to accept or dismiss it. Take some time to consider the information you've been given and whether it holds value for you and your individual goals.

2. **Practice really listening to what the person is saying while resisting the urge to act defensively.**

The best way to practice your active listening skills is by paraphrasing what someone has said to you and repeating it back to them. Make sure you understand what they've said to you correctly.

3. **Change your perception of feedback.**

Try to not think of feedback as "right" or "wrong". Rather see it as useful information you can use to improve yourself, your skills, and your performance.

4. **Avoid seeing someone who gives you feedback as someone who's "out to get you".**

When someone takes the time to give you feedback that can help you improve, it usually means they care about your growth. If someone didn't care about you, they wouldn't bother. I know it can be easy for our fragile egos to feel hurt by someone who is telling us we need to get better at something. But try and see it for what it is. They're trying to help you.

5. **Learn to say "thank you."**

This usually comes with maturity. Especially if you're still stuck in that place of feeling hurt because someone gave you some constructive feedback when you felt like you were doing it on an Olympic level. Just remember that they are trying to help you. Thank them for their feedback and for wanting to help you get better. [24]

We now know that setbacks and failures are important to our growth and that we get to choose our attitude toward the feedback we're given by the people in our lives. When you start embracing mistakes and failures as important tools that will help you grow as an individual, the world is your oyster. You also set yourself free to really go after the goals you want to achieve. In time, the actual goal becomes a focus on the journey, rather than the destination.

What we learn along the way is far more valuable than the actual goal we attain. Learn to fall in love with the journey. With wanting to always improve. Thank the people who give you feedback and help direct you to where you want to go along the way.

You'll be one step closer to becoming a growth mindset master.

EXERCISE:

Think of some feedback you received from a teacher, a coach, or your parents lately. Write down what that feedback was and how it made you feel?

_____

_____

_____

_____

Now, having just gone through the lessons in this chapter, how has your perception of this feedback changed? Do you think it was valuable information? Write down how you will react differently in future when someone gives you constructive feedback. Identify some key areas in your reactions and attitude that you think you need to change.

_____

_____

_____

_____

Here's an easy way to remember how to accept feedback (both compliments and criticism) with a growth mindset.

LOOK	NOD	DON'T ARGUE
THINK	RESTATE	THANK
DECIDE		

CHAPTER 6

EMOTION REGULATION & STRESS MANAGEMENT

"No one can control you when you are in control of yourself"

UNDERSTANDING STRESS AND THE IMPACT IT HAS ON OUR BODY/MIND

Stress is something that can have a detrimental effect on both our bodies and our mind. Stress is the thing that triggers the body's fight/flight/freeze/fawn response. In Chapter 2 we covered some basic information relating to your brain, the different structures in your brain, and their functions.

Now when a stress response is triggered in your body it signals the release of the two stress hormones, namely cortisol and adrenaline. These hormones signal to the body that it needs to get ready to react to whatever is happening. At that moment a number of things are going on inside of your body. Oxygenated blood gets redirected from your organs to your main muscle groups, your heart, and your lungs. This gives you the backup you need to either run away or stand up and fight whatever has triggered this response. Your heart rate goes up and you start taking faster, more shallow breaths to allow as much oxygen as possible to enter your body. Blood is being pumped at an insane rate through your veins and arteries as your body gets ready to react.

This is a perfectly normal reaction in us humans. In most animals in fact. It's a method that our brains and bodies have developed over millions of years to allow us to defend ourselves.

It's this response we've developed that has allowed us to survive all these millions of years and evolve into the modern human beings that we are today.

Though, the tools we needed all those millions of years ago are not the same tools we need to survive in this modern world we live in today. Things have changed. A lot!

We no longer live in caves. We don't have to depend on our hunter-and-gatherer skills to obtain the food we need to survive. We no longer have to be on the lookout for a saber-toothed tiger or wooly mammoth that might kill us.

Today, survival on planet Earth looks very different.

Instead of saber-toothed tigers and wooly mammoths, we need to be on the lookout for bullies, sexual predators, criminals, and terrorists. Instead of bad hygiene or an infection killing us because medicine doesn't exist anymore, we need to be ready for pandemics and superbugs that can wipe out millions of people.

I'd say that our challenges are more emotional today than ever before. Yes, there are still many physical threats that we need to be aware and careful of, but with the internet and social media, emotional threats have become far more prevalent.

The problem that we face is that it took our brains millions of years to evolve into what it is now. It took us only a few thousand years to evolve into the age of technology. So for millions and millions of years, nothing happened, nothing happened, nothing happened, and then BOOM, cities, cars, technology.

Our brains haven't really had time to catch up, have they? So the stress response we developed over the last few million years is still the same response we experience today when our nervous system is triggered.

Our nervous systems have to face different challenges today compared to our great, great, great, great, great, great grandparents. It's a sensory onslaught on a daily basis. Noise cities, noisy people, electronics, polluted air, bright lights, cyberbullying, mental illness; constant stress basically.

Every time your nervous system senses "potential" danger, it releases those stress hormones - cortisol and adrenaline - into your system. Your body's growth processes and your reproductive, digestive, and immune systems are temporarily almost put on hold so the rest of your body can tend to what's more important; your survival! In the good old cave days, those chemicals would work their way out of our bodies by us running or fighting off a mammoth. Nowadays, because we don't have a wooly mammoth to fight off but rather a cyber bully that's triggering our stress response, your body remains in a constant state of high alert. When the stress hormones don't get to leave your body, it causes inflammation and suppresses your immune system which ultimately causes some or other illnesses.

There are so many stress-related illnesses that exist today thanks to our modern lifestyles. Modern does not necessarily mean improved. Here are 9 (out of many) illnesses that can be caused by chronic stress:

Chronic
Stress

1. Insomnia	2. Depression	3. Anxiety and other mental health disorders.
4. Cardiovascular disease.	5. Common cold.	6. Obesity
7. Gastrointestinal disease.	8. Autoimmune diseases.	9. Hypertension (high blood pressure)
10. Cancer		

There are many more, but this is just a short list to demonstrate the devastating effects that stress can have on us. It can make us physically ill.

It's not all doom and gloom though. Stress also has a positive aspect to it. That anxious feeling you get before an exam? That's a stress response. And in this instance, it's a good thing as it can help you perform better.

THE NEGATIVE IMPACT OF STRESS

ON YOUR BODY	ON YOUR MOOD	ON YOUR BEHAVIOR
Headache	Anxiety	Over - or under eating
Muscle tension or pain	Restlessness	Angry outbursts
Chest pain	Lack of motivation or focus	Drug or alcohol misuse
Fatigue	Feeling overwhelmed	Tobacco use
Change in sex drive	Irritability or anger	Social withdrawal
Stomach upset	Sadness or depression	Exercising less often

Taking into consideration the preceding information and looking at the table above, it's pretty clear that stress can have a negative effect on all the different systems in your body, no matter if it's musculoskeletal (muscles and skeleton), respiratory, cardiovascular, your endocrine system (different glands in the body that secrete different hormones), gastrointestinal, nervous, and your reproductive system.

HERE ARE A FEW EXAMPLES OF ACTIVITIES YOU CAN ENGAGE IN TO COUNTER STRESS:

Get in some regular exercise. This can be anything from hitting the gym, running, swimming, and playing sports to taking a walk in nature.

Work some deep relaxation techniques into your daily routine. Exercises like yoga, meditation, and mindfulness can really help counter the effects that stress and inflammation has on the body.

Learn to laugh more and don't take yourself too seriously.

Spend more time with the people that you love and people who make you feel good. Especially those who make you laugh a lot.

Spend more time pursuing your hobbies, e.g. music, art, reading, etc.

Make more time for yourself and your self-care on a regular basis.

Less screen time.

Getting enough sleep is crucial.

Eating a healthy diet. Getting lots of fruits and vegetables.

Journaling regularly to get all those stressful thoughts out onto paper and out of your body.

Talk to someone you trust. This can be a parent, a friend, a teacher, a counselor, etc.

Educate yourself. There are so many free resources on the internet that can help you learn more about how to get rid of the stress inside of your body, as well as dealing with stress on a psychological and emotional level.[25]

1. What are some other things you can think of that you can do to help counter the stress you experience in your life?

_____

_____

_____

_____

2. Looking at the list above, combined with your own, write down how and when you're going to work these activities into your daily life?

_____

_____

_____

_____

Someone with a ***fixed mindset*** will tend to strive for perfectionism. This usually causes a huge amount of unnecessary stress in one's life. The underlying emotion behind perfectionism is *fear*. Fear of making a mistake. Fear of being shot down. Fear of not being good enough. Fear of being rejected. That's what makes us strive to do things just right, and why everything needs to be perfect.

Let's face it, it's easy to see how this can lead to burnout. Imagine how exhausting it must be to always have to do everything perfectly. Maybe you feel this way. Perhaps you feel that if you don't achieve perfection that you will be reprimanded by your parents or teachers. Or maybe it's a case of trying to keep up with some of your peers.

It's tempting to see perfectionism as a positive quality. Though, in reality, there's no such thing as perfect. As human beings, we're all flawed. We make mistakes. We mess up sometimes. And that's okay. It's okay to not be perfect. The Japanese have this concept called "*Kintsugi.*" It is a method of putting back together a broken bowl or pot using golden glue. The end result is quite beautiful and the lesson in this method is to embrace the beauty of human flaws.

Obsessive perfectionism causes a great deal of stress and inflammation in the body which then causes a number of other illnesses, like the ones I listed earlier. Social media has made us buy into this lie that everyone's lives are perfect. That's mostly what you see on the channels you follow right? Happy people with beautiful bodies who seem to have it all. In reality they too have so many of their own struggles. But because all we see is this facade of perfection, that's what we strive for ourselves. Let me tell you, it's a one way ticket to a lifetime of unhappiness.

Life is meant to have its ups and downs. It's the natural order of things. Sometimes you'll get it right, other times you'll get it horribly wrong. Sometimes you'll feel on top of the world, other times you'll feel like you're a complete failure. When we hold on to this idea of needing to get everything right all the time, we place so much stress on ourselves to obtain the unobtainable. It's not worth it.

Yes, it's good to strive to do your best. It's important to work hard. It's important to want to do as well as you possibly can. That's awesome. What's more important is that you accept failure as part of the human experience.

When you embrace a **growth mindset**, you do just that. You know that failure is inevitable. Not just that, failure is something you celebrate as you know that with each failure that comes along you will get to learn something. You'll get better at a certain skill. You'll progress as a human being.

With a growth mindset you strive for excellence, but learn how to remain calm when you fail or run into some unexpected twists and turns along the journey. This helps to release that stress and tension that comes with striving for perfection. It's a more healthy and balanced way of living and can save you a lot of pain and doctor's bills.

You can also substitute the words growth mindset and fixed mindset for "adaptive perfectionism" and "maladaptive perfectionism." Now as we know, anything with "mal" as a prefix is not good. "*Malware, malfunction, malignant, malnutrition, malpractice, etc.*" In some languages the word "*mal*" means "*crazy.*" I think that's a great way of remembering that "*maladaptive perfectionism*" (fixed mindset) will just about drive you crazy.

Maladaptive perfectionists tend to exhibit some or all of the following behaviors:

- Extremely high, unrealistic expectations.
- Giving up on tasks or activities when they feel like they can't win at it, or be the "best" at it.
- Making a mistake means you're a failure. They'll tend to try and hide any mistakes they make because they feel ashamed.
- Spending a lot of time on making sure a project or task is done "perfectly."
- They don't like taking risks unless they know for sure that the outcome will be a good one for them.
- They are overly concerned with what other people think of them and fear that if they show any signs of imperfection they'll be rejected.
- Extremely sensitive to criticism and feedback. They take it very personally.
- They're usually overly critical of others as well.
- If things don't go exactly to plan they tend to feel really stressed out and anxious.
- They have to always do everything themselves because they don't believe others can do it as well, or to the quality level they'd like.

MALADAPTIVE PERFECTIONISTS BEHAVIORS

Just reading through that is enough to get one's stress levels up.

It's natural to want to look good, impress others, and show people what we're made of. That's good. It's called ambition, and a dose of healthy ambition will take you far in life. It's just like anything else in life: "too much of anything isn't good for anyone."

You want to rather strive for adaptive perfectionism, if you strive for perfectionism at all. An adaptive perfectionist strives to develop their skills on a continuous basis. They strive to "adapt" to whatever life throws at them, learn from it, grow as a person, and do better at life. That just sounds way healthier, doesn't it? [26]

HOW TO NOTICE STRESS EARLY ON

Stress doesn't always look the same way. Sometimes it can manifest in ways that we wouldn't consider stress to be the cause. It can be pretty sneaky and insidious. It's important to catch it out early on so you can do something about it. The earlier you can identify stress and the ways it influences your life, the better. This way you can immediately implement strategies to counter that stress and keep yourself healthy.

Like we've seen in the table in this chapter earlier on, stress can manifest physically, emotionally, and psychologically.

Remember the fight/flight/freeze response we spoke about? And remember that Cortisol and Adrenaline are the two stress hormones? So whenever the stress response is activated by an outside force (like a fight or someone shouting at you or someone bullying you) that natural instinct of yours kicks in. But because this is modern-day Earth and not prehistoric Earth, your fight/flight responses might look different.

FIGHT RESPONSE	• Moodiness, irritability. • Bullying others. • Picking fights. • Making trouble in class. • Defiant behavior. • Destructive behavior.
FLIGHT RESPONSE	• Self-isolating. • Not having any friends because you feel like you can't trust anyone. • People who feel anxious engaging in class. • Always trying to find a place where you can be alone. • Not engaging socially. • Always in your room.

FREEZE RESPONSE	• Struggle standing up for yourself. • Feel embarrassed when called upon in class. • Unable to speak in front of others. • Also preferring to be alone.
FAWN RESPONSE	• Going along with something even when you know it's wrong because you don't want to cause any trouble. • Trying to be friends with bullies so they won't turn on you. • Complimenting people only so they'll leave you alone in general. • Unable to stand up for yourself, always giving in to others.

How stress can make you behave:

- Struggling to make decisions/ indecisiveness.
- Experiencing difficulty concentrating.
- Lapses in memory or struggling to recall certain details.
- Having a "short fuze" or easily snapping at people.
- Scratching yourself or picking at your skin, or pulling out hair.
- Cutting yourself.
- Clenching your jaw and/or grinding your teeth.
- Binge eating or eating too little.
- Crying easily, feeling highly emotional all the time.
- Using shopping as a way to self-soothe.
- Using recreational drugs as a way to self-soothe.
- Not moving around or exercising much or at all.
- Isolating yourself.

How stress can make you feel:

- Overwhelmed or anxious.
- Impatient or irritable on a regular basis.
- Nervous or on edge.
- Racing thoughts. Struggling to switch off.
- Depressed.
- Feeling like you've lost interest in life.
- Feeling like you don't have a sense of humor anymore.
- A sense of dread, like something really bad is going to happen.
- Incessant worrying.
- Lonely or isolated.

When you notice any of these symptoms it might be because you're feeling stressed out about something. It could be something like an upcoming exam, a project at school, relationship issues with a friend, crush, or adult, or so many other things. It's important that you be able to quiet down that inner chatter and constant racing thoughts you might be experiencing to tap into your intuition and listen to your body.[27]

A great way to do this is to implement tools like journaling, meditating, and mindfulness into your routine.

Contrary to popular belief, journaling is not just for girls and this is not a "Dear Diary" moment. Journaling is a tool used by counselors, psychologists, and psychiatrists the world over to help their clients and patients deal with many different mental health difficulties.

We think more than 6 000 thoughts a day. Some scientists believe that some of us may have as many as 20 000 thoughts that race through our minds a day. Now of course you can't give each individual thought the same amount of attention. You'd never make it through the day. Your mind is constantly filtering through these thoughts, deciding what is important and what is not, what needs attention and what doesn't.

Over time, and especially when we're stressed out, those thoughts and the feelings associated with them start building up inside of us. It builds up and builds up and builds up until one day when it all blows up. This is usually when we have an emotional meltdown, or get physical with other kids, or do something to harm ourselves.

Journaling is a tool that can help take all those thoughts and emotions that you experience on a daily basis and transfer it onto paper. It's like a daily stress download. You can do it on a tablet, a laptop, or even your phone as well. After a while, this will serve as a great resource that will provide you with invaluable information like:

- Certain triggers in your life that stress you out.

- Certain people who make you feel bad or stressed out. These are the people we want to avoid if possible.

- Maybe there are certain times in a month when the stress builds up. Maybe during tests or exams?

- An indicati

It can also be that "someone" you are able to tell anything to without being judged. on of feelings you seem to have on a regular basis.

EXERCISE

Get yourself a journal or a journaling app that you can set reminders on. For the next week, aim to journal every day at the end of your day before you go to bed. Here are some journaling prompts to help you get started:

- Is there someone who's really stressing you out at the moment? Who is it and why?

- Write about something that happened to you during the day that made you feel stressed out.

- How do you notice your body reacts to stress? How do you know when you are stressed?

- What do you think are some of your personal triggers when it comes to feeling stressed?

- Write down different tools and strategies you can use to help you deal with the stress you're experiencing.

- Write about the frustrations you're experiencing. Who or what is causing you to feel this way and why?

MINDFULNESS MEDITATION EXERCISE:

Mindfulness has been shown to hold a whole bunch of benefits ranging from better concentration, better mood regulation, increased performance overall, and so much more. Here's a simple mindfulness exercise for you to try out. In the notes section after the exercise, write down how you are feeling right now. Then notice any changes after you've completed the exercise and write those down as well.

Start by finding a place where you won't be interrupted. Maybe put on some noise cancelling headphones if you have a pair. You can do this either sitting up or lying down, it doesn't matter. You just need to feel comfortable.

Now close your eyes and just focus on your breathing. Breathe in and out as you normally do. Just keep focusing on your breath for 10 counts or so. Then, start focusing on breathing in deeply through your nose, and out through your mouth. You want it to be long, slow breaths. In through your nose, out through your mouth. Imagine cool blue air going in through your nose as you breathe in, and warm orange air going out through your mouth as you exhale.

Your thoughts will start to wander at some point. That's perfectly normal. Notice them like clouds in the sky that are just passing overhead. Then gently bring your attention back to your breathing. Everytime you notice your attention drifting away just gently guide it back again without any judgment. It's perfectly normal for your mind to want to wander.

Try and do this for 5 minutes to start off with on a daily basis. Then work your way up to 20 - 30 minutes.

Note down how you felt before and after the exercise. Also, make a note of when you plan on doing this exercise on a daily basis. Try and do it consistently for at least a week, then come back to your notes and write down any other changes you may have noticed.

NOTES:

_____

_____

_____

_____

_____

_____

_____

_____

_____

_____

_____

Many mindfulness exercises are based on using our senses to ground ourselves in the present moment. There is a saying that anxiety comes from living in the future (stressing about future events or things that haven't even happened yet) and that depression comes from living in the past. Grounding techniques like this one can help calm down any stress or anxiety you are experiencing by bringing your focus back to the present moment, here and now. It simply works like this:

You can do this absolutely anywhere at any time without anyone even knowing you're doing it. Which is why this is my personal go-to exercise for when I'm feeling stressed out or experiencing high levels of anxiety, an anxiety attack, or a panic attack.

You're going to use 5 of your senses for this exercise.

- Start off by identifying and focusing on 5 things you can see in your immediate environment. Describe it to yourself in your mind in terms of shape and color.

- Now focus on 4 things you can hear around you.

- 3 Things you can touch/feel. Like your clothes, hair, or other objects around you. Describe to yourself what the texture of these things feels like in your mind.

- 2 things you can smell.

- 1 thing you can taste.

 Tip: Smell is a great sense to focus on when you're feeling very anxious or stressed out. You can carry something that you like the smell of with you whenever you're feeling panicky. This can be perfume, essential oils, or whatever you can think of.

Write down some ideas of how you usually deal with the stress in your life. Do you think the strategies you're currently using are healthy, and why or why not? Then make a list of some healthy tools you think you can use to help release the stress in your body and hope you cope better.

NOTES:

Asking for help when we need it is something that very few of us are good at. It can be extremely difficult for some of you to reach out to someone when you're having a hard time. If you're a boy, you've probably been taught to "man up" or "toughen up" and not to cry. Crying is only for girls. Well, it isn't and hopefully you'll learn that now before struggling with it later in life.

Asking for help when you need it is probably the most courageous thing anyone can do. Putting your hand up and saying: "I'm struggling, I please need help." takes more inner strength and courage than you can imagine.

We struggle with it because we don't want to seem weak. It's such a paradox. We don't want to seem weak, but asking for help takes the most courage.

Think of it this way. If your best friend was going through a really hard time and struggling with stress and anxiety, or whatever the case may be, and they felt like they were hitting rock bottom and didn't know what to do, would you want them to reach out to someone and ask for help? Would you want to see them get help?

Of course you would. You'd want what's best for your friend. So why not want that for yourself? You wouldn't judge the people you love for seeking out help when they need it. I can promise you that the people who matter in your life also won't judge you. They'd be happy that you're looking after yourself.

You need to muster up the courage to ask for help when you need it. We all need help at some point in our lives. I've needed help plenty of times in my life. And that's okay.

So if you ever feel like you're down in the dumps, really stressed out, or just really struggling emotionally - please reach out to someone. You deserve to be helped and taken care of.

If you don't know where to start, ask to see the school counselor. Or talk to your parents if you have that kind of relationship where you feel like you can. Open up to a friend. Talk to a teacher, or you can phone a free helpline. Help is always available. You just have to ask.

Our brains have naturally evolved to focus more on the negative than the positive in our lives. This is mainly because it's wired to be on a constant lookout for anything that might be potentially harmful to us. We don't get taught this in school, (or very few people do) so we have to take it upon ourselves to counter this natural reaction, otherwise our nervous systems get stuck in a state of anxiety and/or depression because of all this stress building up inside of us.

A really simple exercise that has truly changed my life for the better is practicing gratitude on a daily basis.

Let me ask you, how often do you reflect on the blessings in your life? On the beauty that surrounds you on a daily basis? Or just how fortunate you are to be alive? Once a day? Once a week? Maybe every now and again? Do you ever take out time to focus on any of these things? And if you don't, why not? You can't tell me it's because you don't have the time, because practicing gratitude can literally just take less than a minute at a time. Or even if it takes 5 minutes. I'm sure you have 5 minutes somewhere in your day where you can focus on the things you're grateful for.

Why should we practice gratitude?

It goes hand-in-hand with having a growth mindset. That, and numerous studies have shown that practicing gratitude on a regular basis holds a number of health benefits.

Gratitude **can**

Help you feel more joy in life.	Increase your sense of satisfaction in life.	Uplift your mood.
Counter symptoms of anxiety and depression.	Help you have a more positive outlook in life.	Improve your sleep.
Boost your immune system.	Build overall resilience.	Decrease chronic pain and risk of disease. [28]

I mean with benefits like those, sign me up! I signed up to practice gratitude on a daily basis years ago in my life. There are many ways in which you can practice gratitude. However you choose to do it, I suggest you do it every single day. It doesn't take much time or effort and can really make a huge difference in your life.

It primes our brains to focus more on the positive stuff in life. This way it starts seeking out more positive stuff. Where your focus goes, energy follows. So when you're constantly focusing on being grateful for the blessings you have in your life, what do you think will happen? You'll receive even more blessings.

There's always something to be grateful for. Even if you feel like you're at the lowest of low levels in your life, there's always still something to be grateful for.

Here are a few exercises you can try to see which works best for you.

MY EXERCISE:

Mine is quite simple. Every night, when I get into bed, I take a moment to think about and list all the things I'm grateful for in my life. It usually only takes a few minutes. To start off with, you can just list 3 things you're grateful for each day. Try and list different things from your day each time.

Write down 3 things you are grateful for today:

Write a gratitude letter:

For this exercise, you're going to write a letter to someone expressing your gratitude for something they've done that helped you in some way, or that had a positive impact on you.

It can be to a friend who helped you out with some homework or a project. To your parents, to a teacher. It doesn't matter who it is.

It might feel a bit awkward, but it's like giving someone a gift. Imagine if you got a letter from someone you care about out of the blue, telling you how grateful they are for you.

You don't have to limit yourself to just one letter. You can write as many as you want.

Who are you going to write to and what are you going to thank them for?

Consider your blessings:

We often take for granted just how blessed we are in life. With so much poverty and suffering in other parts of the world, the mere fact that you have a bed to sleep in is something to be grateful for.

For this exercise, consider what other kids don't have and write down a list of things you're grateful for in your life. Come back to this list often to remind yourself to show more gratitude for all the blessings in your life.

PROBLEM-SOLVING SKILLS

We all need problem-solving skills in life. At some point, you will run into a problem that needs solving. I'm not just talking about math problems here, I mean problems and challenges in life that will need solving as you get older.

These skills are important, not only in your professional life but in your personal life as well. People often only think of problem-solving skills in terms of the challenges they face at work. Though you will undoubtedly face problems and challenges within your relationships as well. If those relationships are important to you, you'll want to find a solution that works for all parties involved.

Problem-solving motivates us to find creative solutions to obstacles in life and is a key skill needed for someone with a growth mindset. When you're solving problems, it's important to be able to:

- Listen carefully and think calmly.

- Consider all the options available to you and respect other people's opinions and needs as well.

- Negotiate for what you want, whilst also finding a way to give the other person what they want as well. It's called compromising.

Here are 6 steps you can follow to become a master problem solver.

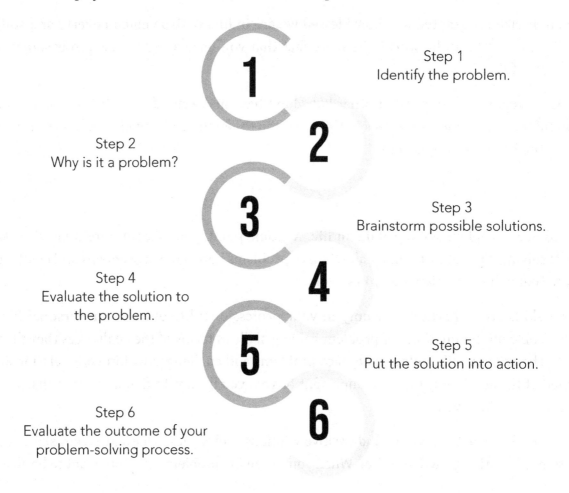

Step 1
Identify the problem.

Step 2
Why is it a problem?

Step 3
Brainstorm possible solutions.

Step 4
Evaluate the solution to
the problem.

Step 5
Put the solution into action.

Step 6
Evaluate the outcome of your
problem-solving process.

STEP 1: IDENTIFY THE PROBLEM.

Before you can solve a problem you need to be able to identify and understand the problem. Especially when the problem involves more than one person. You want to make sure that everyone understands the problem and that everyone's on the same page.

STEP 2: WHY IS IT A PROBLEM?

This means describing the cause of the problem and where it's coming from. Consider asking yourself questions like

- Why is this so important to me?

- What might happen if I don't solve this?

- Why do I feel like I need this?

E.g. Let's say you and your brother are arguing over who gets to play on the Xbox. You want to play an online tournament game with your friends, and so does your brother. Consider the questions above and think about ways you can compromise in this situation so you both get time on the Xbox.

STEP 3: BRAINSTORM POSSIBLE SOLUTIONS.

Make a list of possible solutions that you can explore together, or on your own if the problem only pertains to you.

E.g. Maybe you and your brother can compromise and agree on a schedule that determines who gets to play on the Xbox. Or you can figure out a way to make some pocket money to buy your own Xbox? There's always a solution.

STEP 4: EVALUATE THE SOLUTION TO THE PROBLEM.

Draw up a pros and cons list of all the different possible solutions. What are the pros of taking turns versus the cons? What are the pros of saving up to buy your own tv and Xbox vs the cons?

Maybe the pros of the last option are that you never have to worry about sharing an Xbox again. The cons are that it'll take some time before you get to the point where you've saved up enough money to buy your own. So it might make more sense to settle for option one at this stage.

STEP 5: PUT THE SOLUTION INTO ACTION.

You and your brother sit down and draw up a schedule that you can agree on. So in this case it might be that you both agree to take turns for an hour at a time.

STEP 6: EVALUATE THE OUTCOME OF YOUR PROBLEM-SOLVING PROCESS.

This is where you evaluate whether the solution you came up with has worked or not. If, after a while, you both realize that this one-hour-at-a-time solution isn't working, you may need to renegotiate and agree on two hours at a time, etc.

Within the framework of a growth strategy, this fits right in as it allows you to assess what you need to do, implement any changes that might need addressing, then learn from the process you've just gone through. [29]

Having to deal with and manage stress is a part of life. It's something you'll face on a daily basis at different times of your life as you move from one stage in life to the next. There will always be stress and obstacles that we need to face, it's a fact. By reminding yourself and implementing some of the skills you've learned in this chapter, you will be able to remain more calm in life and practice more control over your emotions. This will certainly serve you in the long run as you're then able to make decisions that are in your best interest instead of giving in to a knee-jerk reaction based on what you're feeling at any given moment.

In the next chapter, we'll be exploring all things goal setting.

CHAPTER 7

GOAL SETTING

"If you want to be happy in life, tie it to a goal. Not to people or things." - Albert Einstein

---

TURNING VAGUE GOALS INTO STRATEGIC SMART GOALS

It's important for us to have goals in life. Not having goals is like traveling towards a destination, except you don't know where it is or how you're supposed to get there. It's your compass and guide in life.

Our goals are usually based on things that relate to who we want to be, what we want in life, what we want to feel, and what we want to achieve. Working hard is great, but working hard without knowing what you're wanting or are supposed to achieve won't get you anywhere. Then it's just a whole lot of time and energy wasted on working hard to stand still essentially. Not very helpful, is it?

What's even more important than having goals is making sure that your goals are SMART goals. Now, when I say SMART, I don't mean the way I would if I was referring to intellect. In this sense, the word "SMART" is an acronym that stands for:

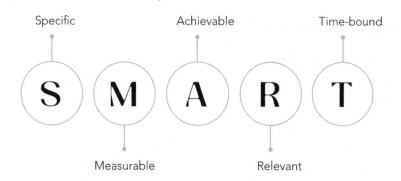

SPECIFIC

You want your goal to be specific, simple, sensible, and significant. If your goal is too broad or too abstract like: "I want to be happy," then you risk working hard to stand still in one place. Because what does "happy" mean? Happiness can look different to different people. A more specific goal might be to identify *what makes you feel happy*? Let's say that it's hanging out with your best friend. Just the two of you watching movies. With this in mind, a specific goal might sound like: "*I want to spend at least one evening a week with (friend's name) just hanging out and watching movies.*" If you want to improve your grades one of your goals might be: "*I will study for an extra hour every weekday, focusing on one subject a day.*" See, that's specific.

MEASURABLE

This is how you track your progress. So, let's look at the last example I gave you. In this example the measurable part is doing it for *one hour a day, every weekday*. This is the part that makes it measurable. You know that if you stick to one hour a day on weekdays then you're on track to achieving your goal.

ACHIEVABLE

It's important to have goals, but setting goals for yourself that are impossible to achieve will only end up in failure and resentment. You want to make sure that your goal is reasonable and attainable. Going back to our example: one hour a day on weekdays is totally achievable. Had I said that "*I want to put in an extra 5 hours of studying every single day of the week on top of my regular school work and extra mural activities,*" that would've been completely unrealistic and unattainable.

RELEVANT

Is this the right thing for you? You can establish this point by asking yourself the following questions:

- Is this really important to me?

- Is this the right time to try and achieve this?

- Does this align with my values?

- Do I really need this?

- Will achieving this goal be helpful to me or affect my life in a positive way?

Now that you know what the target is, you need to know where it is. That is achieved by setting a target date. You need to know when to hit your target by. You can't study for an extra hour a day every weekday for the rest of your life! To what end? So your SMART goal might look a little something like this:

"I want to go from a C average to a B average this coming semester. To do this I will put in an extra hour of studying on weekdays, setting up a schedule of which subjects I'll be focusing on on which days. I will do this until the end of exams at the end of this semester."

You now know what you want to do, why you want to do it, how you're going to do it, and when you need to do it by. Tada - SMART goal. [30]

Identify ONE major goal you would like to focus on for the next week. Then use the method above to rework it into being a SMART goal. Write it down below and make a promise to yourself to stick to this goal for the next 7 days. Once you get to the end of the next 7 days, come back to this exercise and set a SMART goal for the next month. You can choose the second one now if you want.

_____

_____

_____

_____

_____

_____

_____

Once you know what it is you want to achieve, why it's important to you, how you're going to get there and by when, the next step is to keep regular track of your progress. This way, should you stray from your path, you can correct your heading before you go too far off track. It also helps to see whether what you're doing, in terms of your strategy for achieving your goal, is working.

Some goals may last longer and need more reflection and adjustment along the way, other goals may be more short-term or immediate.

No matter the goal size and length of time though, you need to be able to keep track of your progress. Here are 5 that can help you do this:

Five Tips

1. Break down your goals into smaller tasks.

So instead of having one massive chunk of a goal that might feel a little overwhelming to you, break it up into smaller, more achievable chunks. If your goal will last for 3 months, break it up into weekly segments where, at the end of each week, you look back at what you've achieved and take stock of what you still need to do.

2. Set yourself a reward system.

Once you've broken your task up into different milestones, set a reward for every milestone you reach to keep track of your progress. The reward can be anything really and depends on what you consider to be an award. I'm currently on a health journey and aiming to lose a few pounds. So for every 3 weeks that I go without sugar, I allow myself 1 treat.

3. Keep a daily journal.

This is one of the best ways of keeping track of your goals. This way you can monitor everything related to your goal ranging from the progress you see along the way to the different difficulties you experience. Journaling will also help you identify any key areas that need some attention along the way, such as specific tasks you struggle with and brainstorming how you might do it in an easier or more enjoyable way.

4. Plan ahead.

Knowing what you want to achieve and how is great, but unless you do the necessary preparations in between, you're sure to come face-to-face with some obstacles sooner rather than later. Wanting to spend an extra hour a day studying when you haven't done your other homework first might not be the best way of tackling your goal.

5. There's an App for that.

There are so many goal tracking apps available for you to use. Some of them make it really fun by turning your goals into a role playing game. For every milestone of your goal you achieve, you get points and can buy and do all kinds of cool stuff. It certainly makes it more interesting. Here are some apps for you to check out:

- Habitica
- Coach.me
- Goals on Track
- Goals of Life
- ClickUp

Keeping track of your progress, no matter what you do in life, will always be crucial for determining your success. [31]

It's the same as feedback. When you track your progress you are provided with feedback that allows you to constantly remain informed on how you're doing. Do you need to change something? Whether you're perhaps on the wrong track? Remember, feedback is your friend.

Progress isn't linear. Instead, it is a series of many ups and downs, frustrations and triumphs, tears and laughter along the way. If it were linear and all we had to do is to progress at a steady pace, doing the same thing the same way at the same time everyday, how boring would that be? Well, it depends on who you talk to. I like structure and systems, so I'd love it. But I can bet that the majority of people wouldn't be too keen on the idea. Maybe at first, but after the first few weeks it would feel like it's Groundhog Day, every day. (If you haven't seen that move, it's an old movie starring Bill Murray who is stuck living Groundhog Day over and over again)

On this journey that we call life, you'll experience some success and take a few steps forward, then you might have a small setback and take a step back, you might get to a hurdle which causes you to trip and fall. Then you'll get back up again, learn from what just happened and carry on. This is what I mean with *"progress isn't linear."*

As the late John F Kennedy said: *"Change is the law of life. And those who look only to the past or the present, are certain to miss the future."* [31]

As important as it is for us to have the ability to implement tools like mindfulness and meditation to ground ourselves in the present, especially when we're feeling stressed or overwhelmed, it's also important that we plan ahead. This doesn't mean that you should fixate on the future and what is yet to come. This might just turn into stress and anxiety itself and besides, the future isn't something you can control right now. You can only try to plan for it and adapt and change along the way.

Your life won't get better just by accident or chance. It only gets better through change. When you are resistant to adapting to change, you start leaning towards more of a fixed mindset. Because the only certainty in life is change, this type of mindset guarantees that you'll have a horrible time.

Sometimes you'll be forced to leave the warm, comfortable cocoon that is your comfort zone. It might feel incredibly uncomfortable at first, but it is what helps us learn and get better in life. It is what allows us to build resilience, and resilience is basically your ability to get back up and continue after you've tripped over that hurdle and fell down.

Five Ways

Here are 5 ways in which you can embrace change:

1. Change your mindset

Which has been the main point of this book. Choosing to adopt a growth mindset makes it easier to embrace change. Trying to resist change will just keep you from reaching your highest potential. Like I've said before, you only get one shot at this life, so go for it with all you've got!

2. Find meaning in your life

A very big part of what predicts our happiness is whether we live in line with our life's purpose. Numerous studies have shown that people who don't feel like they have a purpose in life experience greater levels of unhappiness along with conditions like depression. When you feel like you have no purpose in life, you feel like you don't have a reason to be here. And if you don't have a reason to be here, what's the point? But there is a reason why you're here and that reason is called your *purpose.*

3. Let go of your regrets

Regrets can so often hold us back in life. You did something wrong, made a mistake, and now you feel a great deal of regret that can keep you from moving forward. Regret doesn't serve us at all. Yes, it's important that one takes a tally of mistakes you've made and people you may have hurt along the way. But that's feedback that allows us to do better the next time around. Let go of any regrets you hold about anything you might have done in the past. You're not going that way, so stop looking there.

4. Run towards your fears

Write a list of scary things that you've been too afraid to do, then go and do it. Fear is a very powerful emotion that can keep us from doing things we really want to in life. It can keep you from getting that amazing job you've always wanted, or that boy you've had a crush on since middle school. I read about an interview that was conducted, asking over a hundred terminally ill patients what they would've done differently in their lives looking back. The one consistent answer: *"be less afraid."* Fear usually just leads to regret.

5. Live a balanced and healthy life

Without your health, you have nothing. A friend once said that to me when he told me a story about this millionaire he once knew. This multi-millionaire had so much money that he could retire at age 30. But he never looked after his health and partied and drank and smoked too much. Then he got sick. Very sick. He had liver failure from all his drinking. And on his deathbed he said to this friend of mine: *"you can have all the money in the world, but without your health it doesn't mean a thing."* You can have all the goals, work ethic, and best mindset in the world. But without your health, it doesn't mean a thing. Look after your health - that means physically, mentally, spiritually, and emotionally. [32]

EXERCISE

Identify 3 things you're afraid of doing, but actually really want to do. Then come up with a strategy on how and when you're going to do it. Commit to the plan and then execute it. One thing a week over the next three weeks. Write them down below and also the reason why you want to do it.

_____

_____

_____

_____

_____

_____

_____

_____

_____

_____

_____

_____

CHAPTER 8

THE GROWTH MINDSET LIFESTYLE

"Whether you think you can, or think you can't, you're right." - Henry Ford

---

This quote above by Henry Ford is one that really struck me the first time I heard it. Whether you think you can, or think you can't, you're right. It means that you get to choose how far you go in life, or not. It's all up to you. It's your choice and no one else's. It can be hard to hear for some, because it basically means that it's all up to you kid.

At the same time it's extremely good news, because it's all up to you kid. No one can tell you how far you're allowed to go in life or what you're allowed to achieve in life. No matter who you are or where you come from, even if where you come from is covered in trauma, pain, and poverty, the choice is still yours.

Here are 7 tips to help you make sure you stay on track and keep improving on your growth mindset on a daily basis:

Determine where you are currently

Where do you consider yourself to be at this present moment in your life? Do you already have a bit of a growth mindset going on that you'd like to build on, or are you on the opposite end of the field? It's good to first stop and take stock of where you're at so you can determine what you'd like to do next.

Why do you want to develop a growth mindset?

Explore why this is important to you. Someone that has a why to live for can endure almost any "what" that crosses their path. What benefits do you think this will bring you? Knowing what's in it for you always makes it easier to go after something.

Identify others who have developed a growth mindset.

Chat to your friends, parents, and teachers. Ask them if they've heard of this thing called a growth mindset and what their take on it is. Maybe they'll be able to give you some valuable insight and tips to help you on your journey. We can always learn something from others.

Change your perspective on failure.

We've gone over this before, but I believe it is such an important point that I'm including it here again. Say it with me: "Failure is your friend."

Gain an understanding of your own limitations.

I know some of you might feel like you're invisible. Especially at this age. Though we all have our own limitations. You'll get to know more of them as you get older. Recognizing what might be beyond what you can realistically achieve will help you rather focus your energy on something else that you can actually achieve.

Mind your words.

Be mindful of how you talk about yourself, both in your head and in front of others. Swap phrases like "I can't do this" for "I can't do this yet," and "I'll never be able to get this right" for "With time and practice I'll get better." You want to reinforce your growth mindset by constantly reminding yourself that you are constantly learning and improving.

Learn as much as you can about the brain and human behavior.

You now know that your brain is constantly changing and developing. You've learned about neuroplasticity and how you can use it to develop any skill you want. Continuously teaching yourself all there is to know about the world of neuroscience, psychology, and personal development will give you the tools to back up your journey to cultivating the strongest growth mindset you can possibly have.

IMPROVEMENTS YOU'LL SEE OVER TIME

As time goes on and you continue on this journey of yours to harness the power that comes with a growth mindset, you'll start noticing some changes happening in your life. As with anything else in life, it takes some time and effort of course. Rome wasn't built in a day. Anything worth having is worth working for.

Then, one day not too far from now, you'll notice that something's different. Your self-confidence is better than it used to be. Your grades have gone up. Your performance is on a level it's never been before.

Last week you made a mistake when that teacher called on you for an answer, and when the whole class laughed, you laughed with them instead of wanting to climb under your desk and disappear.

You'll start noticing more and more changes happening in your life when you focus on keeping that growth mindset of yours constantly developing and getting stronger. Here's a short list of more benefits you might start noticing:

- You're enjoying your life more, even when it's not perfect and even when you're not perfect.
- An increase in your self-esteem. Feeling better about yourself overall.
- Knowing yourself better than you have before.
- Your relationships are better and stronger than ever.
- Less toxic people in your life.
- You enjoy making mistakes because you know you'll learn from it. You're embracing the suck!
- You don't allow yourself to stress about things you cannot control anymore.
- You also don't allow yourself to stress about having to be perfect anymore. Hooray!
- Your overall mood and zest for life has never been better.
- You're finally taking responsibility for your own life.
- You don't blame others for your mistakes.
- You're more grateful every single day.
- Suddenly more opportunities are showing up in your life.
- You seem to have better resilience when it comes to negative people or bullies.
- You don't allow others opinions of you to affect you as much anymore.
- You face your fears head on.
- You start enjoying putting in the time and effort, knowing that it will lead to progress.
- You're more humble and down to Earth.
- People gravitate towards your positivity.
- You're feeling more optimistic about life in general.

I mean, this is a pretty awesome list don't you think?

It is an awesome list. But it doesn't happen overnight, and it doesn't come for free. You have to put in the work. So let's close this off with some exercises to see you on your journey towards becoming the best version of you that you can possibly be. [33]

DAY-TO-DAY ACTIVITIES TO CULTIVATE A GROWTH MINDSET

1. Read other growth mindset books like this one.

2. Watch TED Ed videos online. There is always much inspiring and educational content out there for you to consume.

3. Fold an origami penguin. Yes, you read that right. Take a piece of paper and try to fold an origami penguin without looking up how to do it. I'll give you a tip at the end of this section. *

4. Look up some words related to a growth mindset. Write or print them out in creative ways and stick them up on your wall so you can see them everyday. Positive, affirmative words like: "Courage, Determination, Strength, Possibility, I Can, I am Worthy, I am Awesome," etc. Make it colorful and fun.

5. Compare the pros and cons of having a growth mindset vs having a fixed mindset for yourself.

6. Focus on the words that enter your mind every single day. If a negative word comes up, catch it, and then replace it with a more positive word.

7. Make the word "YET" your best friend. Whenever you fail or are not able to do something, just say to yourself: "*I just can't do it YET. But I'm learning and I'll get better.*"

8. Play fun puzzle games with your friends where you have to find solutions, both individually and as a team. Try giving one of those escape rooms a go. They're a lot of fun. (As long as you haven't seen the movies)

9. Look up some famous and successful people and failures they experienced in their lives. This will serve as a powerful reminder that mistakes and failures can lead us to the top.

10. Make a spy game out of your failures and mistakes. Investigate them from every angle and open yourself up to curiosity. Try to find different solutions and options you can try out next time.

11. Make a list of new skills you'd like to learn in the next year. Then implement the SMART Goals technique and strategize a way to achieve those goals.

12. Ask your parents to get involved. Ask them to make you aware anytime you talk about yourself or your performance in a negative manner. Do the same with friends and all the other people around you. They can help catch the little negativity monsters that slip through the cracks.

13. Make a list of all the things you're bad at. Then focus on them one at a time, putting in time and effort to get better at those skills.

14. Be more mindful of how you spend your time. Instead of mindlessly scrolling on your phone, listen to an educational podcast. Read a book. Watch a TED video. Learn something.

15. Remember to write in your journal every day. Write about what you're grateful for. Write about what your goals are. Write about what you've learned today. Write about your progress. Write about your mistakes and failures and what you learned from those.

* The origami penguin: you can't do it without knowing how. Now look up a tutorial and try it again. This is a great process to show you that learning how to do something and then getting better at it takes time, effort, and practice.

There's so much information, tools, books, videos, courses, and other content on how to cultivate a growth mindset online. These days there's nothing you can't learn, thanks to the internet. Be curious, about yourself, about life, about other people, all of it. You're only here for a little while. I know it might feel like you're going to be here forever. But you won't.

Learning these kinds of lessons earlier on in life makes it easier to be more resilient and achieve the things you want later in life. It might even help you become the next big thing on YouTube or the next multimillionaire entrepreneur. Whatever your dreams and aspirations, you can achieve it with a growth mindset. There's no such thing as impossible. As cheesy as it might sound, turn that horrible word around and make it "I'm possible."

Just remember, you being here isn't a mistake. You were born against stupendous odds. You were meant to be here. Now make the most of this opportunity. Life is an absolutely amazing experience with so much to see, do, and learn along the way. I sincerely hope that you'll get to go on many adventures.

Wherever life may take you, just remember: failure is your friends. Whether you think you can or you think you can't, you're right. And it's all up to you kid.

On the next page you'll find a 30-day growth mindset challenge. Commit to this challenge for the next 30 days to help transform your mindset and reap the benefits that comes with structure and discipline. It's just 30 days. You can do it!

Now go be awesome!

---

30 DAY GROWTH MINDSET CHALLENGE

Day 1	Day 2	Day 3	Day 4	Day 5
No complaining for the entire day	Write down and transform 3 limiting beliefs	Repeat 3 positive affirmations morning and night	Write down 5 things you're grateful for	Meditate for 20 minutes
Day 6	Day 7	Day 8	Day 9	Day 10
Do a mindfulness exercise	No social media for the entire day	Unfollow negative people and pages	Journal about your goals for the next month	Do something kind for someone else
Day 11	Day 12	Day 13	Day 14	Day 15
Do something that scares you	Write down 3 skills you have that you're proud of	Practice no judgement of other for a day	List 3 positive characteristics about yourself	List 3 things you're proud of
Day 16	Day 17	Day 18	Day 19	Day 20
Ask a role model for advice for success	Write down a lesson you learned from a mistake you made	Write down your definition of success	Watch an inspiring TED Talk	Tidy up your room
Day 21	Day 22	Day 23	Day 24	Day 25
Journal for 10 minutes. Just write down everything that you think of	Write down 3 goals you have for the next 6 months	Focus on identifying beauty in your environment for the day	Write down a list of 3 things you want to improve on in your life	Do some yoga, hit the gym, do some sports, go for a run, etc. Get active
Day 26	Day 27	Day 28	Day 29	Day 30
Listen to music that puts you in a good mood	Say thank you to someone who has been supportive of you	Get at least 8 hours of sleep	List 3 positive things that happened today	No complaining for the entire day

CONCLUSION

I really hope that you have found this book to be interesting and helpful. I hope you've learned something along the way and that you feel inspired to go out there and give it all you've got.

It's taken me years and a lot of mistakes along the way to truly learn just how helpful a growth mindset can be. I wish that someone had taught this to me when I was your age, which is why I sincerely hope that you will take this information and run with it.

The exercises throughout the book are there to help you better learn and understand the content and concept of what a growth mindset is. Please take the time to do these exercises. They're there to help you, but you have to do the work. I can't do it for you.

The next step is to take all you've learned and to implement it into your life on a daily basis. It won't be easy, but with time you'll start reaping the benefits. Believe me, it's absolutely worth it.

Use the extra time and energy you have to learn more about the subjects relating to cultivating a growth mindset and other personal development tools and techniques. These are the skills you will carry with you for the rest of your life.

There will be times when you feel like life is just too hard and that you want to give up. Don't be too hard on yourself. Life is hard. It's the hardest thing you'll ever have to do. But do it well. Embrace all your emotions, but learn how to not allow them to take control of your behavior. Go out and face your fears, but don't do something stupid. Reach for the stars, but also know your own limitations.

Yes, I know I want to say nothing is impossible, but I would like to think I can fly but don't see any cape hanging off my back, so...

Just be 100% authentically you. That's what this world needs. Just beautiful, magnificent you.

SOURCES

Gordon B. Hinkley quote: Brainy Quote (n.d.). *Foundation Quotes*. Retrieved July 10, 2023, from https://www.brainyquote.com/quotes/gordon_b_hinckley_539629?src=t_foundation

[1] https://www.mensa.org/

[2] Brainy Quote (n.d.). *Thomas Edison Quotes*. Retrieved July 11, 2023, from https://www.brainyquote.com/quotes/thomas_a_edison_132683

[3] Forbes Quotes (n.d.). *Thoughts On The Business Of Life*. Retrieved July 11, 2023, from https://www.forbes.com/quotes/11194/

[4] Flatley, K. (n.d.). *8 Fixed Mindset and Growth Mindset Examples and How to Help Kids Improve*. Self Sufficient Kids. Retrieved July 11, 2023, from https://selfsufficientkids.com/growth-mindset-examples-and-fixed-mindset-examples/#h-8-fixed-vs-growth-mindset-examples

[5] Mayfield Brain & Spine (2018, April 1). *Anatomy of the Brain*. Retrieved July 12, 2023, from https://mayfieldclinic.com/pe-anatbrain.htm

Northern Brain Injury Association (n.d.). *Brain Structure And Function*. Retrieved July 12, 2023, from https://www.nbia.ca/brain-structure-function/

[6] Seladi-Schulman, J., PhD. (2018, July 24). *What Part of the Brain Controls Emotions?* Healthline. Retrieved July 12, 2023, from https://www.healthline.com/health/what-part-of-the-brain-controls-emotions#happiness

[7] Harvard University - Psychology Department (n.d.). *Karl Lashley*. Harvard University. Retrieved July 12, 2023, from https://psychology.fas.harvard.edu/people/karl-lashley

[8] University College London (2022, February 1). *London taxi drivers' brains being scanned for Alzheimer's research*. Retrieved July 12, 2023, from https://www.ucl.ac.uk/news/2022/feb/london-taxi-drivers-brains-being-scanned-alzheimers-research

[9] Gage F. H. (2004). Structural plasticity of the adult brain. Dialogues in clinical neuroscience, 6(2), 135-141. Retrieved July 13, 2023, from https://doi.org/10.31887/DCNS.2004.6.2/fgage

[10] Stone, E. (2017, May 8). *Sitting Near a High-Performer Can Make You Better at Your Job*. KELLOGG SCHOOL OF MANAGEMENT AT NORTHWESTERN UNIVERSITY. Retrieved July 13, 2023, from https://insight.kellogg.northwestern.edu/article/sitting-near-a-high-performer-can-make-you-better-at-your-job#:~:text=Researchers%20looked%20at%20the%2025,in%20coworkers%20by%2015%20percent.

[11] Twomey, S. (2010, January 1). *Phineas Gage: Neuroscience's Most Famous Patient*. Smithsonian Magazine. Retrieved July 13, 2023, from https://www.smithsonianmag.com/history/phineas-gage-neurosciences-most-famous-patient-11390067/

[12] Studymaster (n.d.). *Plasticity and Functional Recovery of the Brain After Trauma*. Retrieved July 13, 2023, from https://www.studysmarter.co.uk/explanations/psychology/biopsychology/plasticity-and-functional-recovery-of-the-brain-after-trauma/

Chapter 3 Introduction Quote: https://www.brainyquote.com/quotes/michael_jordan_129404?src=t_roadblocks

[13] Aprianti, V. (2022, December 12). *6 Common Roadblocks to having a Growth Mindset*. Medium. Retrieved July 13, 2023, from https://medium.com/@vivin.apriyanti/6-common-roadblock-to-having-growth-mindset-bb71d5890467

Flynn, D. (n.d.). *The 6 Roadblocks to Success (and How to Remove Them)t*. Convey Club. Retrieved July 13, 2023, from https://www.coveyclub.com/blog_posts/the-6-roadblocks-to-success-and-how-to-remove-them

Chapter 4 Quote: https://www.goodreads.com/quotes/tag/limiting-beliefs

[14] [ThisIs432]. (2012, November 18). *Masaru Emoto - Water Experiments* [Video]. YouTube. https://www.youtube.com/watch?v=1qQUFvufXp4

[15] Footprints to Recovery (n.d.). *7 Ways to Combat Negative Self-Talk*. Retrieved July 18, 2023, from https://footprintstorecovery.com/blog/combat-negative-self-talk/

[16] Star, K., PhD. (2022, March 9). *How to Stop Jumping to Conclusions*. Verywell Mind. Retrieved July 18, 2023, from https://www.verywellmind.com/jumping-to-conclusions-2584181

Therapy Now SF (2020, December 30). *JUMPING TO CONCLUSIONS: LEARN HOW TO STOP MAKING ANXIETY-FUELED MENTAL LEAPS.* Retrieved July 18, 2023, from https://www.therapynowsf.com/blog/jumping-to-conclusions-learn-how-to-stop-making-anxiety-fueled-mental-leaps

[17] Tony Robbins (n.d.). *WHERE FOCUS GOES, ENERGY FLOWS.* Retrieved July 18, 2023, from https://www.tonyrobbins.com/career-business/where-focus-goes-energy-flows/

[18] Bokhari, D. (2020, November 26). *How to Develop a Can Do Attitude and Succeed in Life.* Retrieved July 18, 2023, from https://www.lifehack.org/833809/can-do-attitude

Puak Jovanovic, S. (n.d.). *7 Ways To Develop a Can-Do Attitude.* Happiness.com. Retrieved July 18, 2023, from https://www.happiness.com/magazine/personal-growth/seven-ways-to-develop-a-can-do-attitude/

[19] Moore, C., MBA (2019, June 2). *How to Practice Self-Compassion: 8 Techniques and T.* Positive Psychology. Retrieved July 18, 2023, from https://positivepsychology.com/how-to-practice-self-compassion/#8-tips-and-techniques-for-practicing-self-compassion

Neff, K., Dr. (n.d.). *Self Compassion.* Self Compassion.org. Retrieved July 18, 2023, from https://self-compassion.org/the-three-elements-of-self-compassion-2/

[20] Psych Central (2014, October 30). *5 Tips for Changing Negative Self Beliefs.* Retrieved July 18, 2023, from https://psychcentral.com/blog/5-tips-for-changing-negative-self-beliefs#4

Chapter 5 Introductory Quote: Good Reads (n.d.). *Failure Quotes.* Retrieved July 18, 2023, from https://www.goodreads.com/quotes/tag/failure

[21] Vajello, M., LCSW. (2023, March 17). *How Do Students With a Growth Mindset See Their Mistakes?* Mental Health Center for Kids. Retrieved July 19, 2023, from https://mentalhealthcenterkids.com/blogs/articles/how-do-students-with-a-growth-mindset-see-their-mistakes

[22] (n.d.). *Dr. Seuss.* Good Reads Quotes. Retrieved July 19, 2023, from https://www.goodreads.com/quotes/3160-today-you-are-you-that-is-truer-than-true-there

[23] (n.d.). *How to Accept (and Embrace) Imperfection.* Hudson Therapy Group. Retrieved July 19, 2023, from https://hudsontherapygroup.com/blog/how-to-accept-and-embrace-imperfection

[24] Sound Physicians (2018, October 24). *5 Tips for Being Receptive to Feedback.* Retrieved July 20, 2023, from https://soundphysicians.com/blog/5-tips-for-being-receptive-to-feedback/

[25] Mayo Clinic (2021, March 24). *Stress symptoms: Effects on your body and behavior.* Retrieved July 25, 2023, from https://www.mayoclinic.org/healthy-lifestyle/stress-management/in-depth/stress-symptoms/art-20050987

[26] Mind Tools (n.d.). *Perfectionism.* Retrieved July 25, 2023, from https://www.mindtools.com/a4jvsqi/perfectionism

[27] Mind.org.uk (2022, March 1). *Stress.* Mind. Retrieved July 25, 2023, from https://www.mind.org.uk/information-support/types-of-mental-health-problems/stress/signs-and-symptoms-of-stress/

[28] Scott, E., PhD (2021, March 22). *Cultivate Gratitude and Feel Happier With Life.* Verywell Mind. Retrieved July 26, 2023, from https://www.verywellmind.com/cultivate-gratitude-and-feel-happier-with-life-3144864

Eichenseher, T. (2022, April 4). *6 Ways to Be More Grateful and Why It Is Worth It.* Psych Central. Retrieved July 26, 2023, from https://psychcentral.com/blog/how-to-be-more-grateful-exercises#benefits

[29] Little, E. (2021, May 11). *Problem-solving steps: Pre-teens and teenagers.* Raising Children. Retrieved July 26, 2023, from https://raisingchildren.net.au/pre-teens/behaviour/encouraging-good-behaviour/problem-solving-steps

[30] Mind Tools Team (n.d.). *SMART Goals.* Mind Tools. Retrieved July 26, 2023, from https://www.mindtools.com/a4wo118/smart-goals

[31] Influencive (2019, May 28). *NINE EFFECTIVE WAYS TO TRACK YOUR PROGRESS TOWARD A GOAL.* Retrieved July 26, 2023, from https://www.influencive.com/nine-effective-ways-to-track-your-progress-toward-a-goal/

[32] Sandford, K. (2021, January 12). *Adapting to Change: Why It Matters and How to Do It.* Life Hack. Retrieved July 26, 2023, from https://www.lifehack.org/372463/why-you-need-adapt-change

[33] Alex Vermeer (2012, April 1). *15 Benefits of the Growth Mindset.* Retrieved July 26, 2023, from https://alexvermeer.com/15-benefits-growth-mindset/

Made in the USA
Coppell, TX
19 November 2024

40584803R00063